PUFFIN BOOKS

TALES OF ANCIENT EGYPT

Roger Lancelyn Green begins this collection of the legends of Egypt with the story of Amen-Ra, the father of gods and men who created all the creatures of the world, and follows it with the story of how faithful Isis searched the waters for the body of her dead husband, Osiris. Here, too, you will find the legends concerning the source of the Nile; Se-Osiris, the boy magician, and his journey to the land of the dead; and about sea-serpents, and the fate of lovely Helen.

This book, told with the clarity and scholarship which made Roger Lancelyn Green's tales of Greece and Troy so memorable, breaks fresh ground for everyone who enjoys myths and legends, with plenty of new stories.

For boys and girls of nine and over.

TALES OF ANCIENT EGYPT

Selected and retold by

ROGER LANCELYN GREEN

Illustrations by Heather Copley

PUFFIN BOOKS
in association with The Bodley Head

Puffin Books, Penguin Books Ltd, Harmondsworth, Middlesex, England
Viking Penguin Inc., 40 West 23rd Street, New York 10010, U.S.A.
Penguin Books Australia Ltd, Ringwood, Victoria, Australia
Penguin Books Canada Limited, 2801 John Street, Markham, Ontario, Canada L3R 1B4
Penguin Books (N.Z.) Ltd, 182–190 Wairau Road, Auckland 10, New Zealand

—

First published by The Bodley Head 1967
Published in Puffin Books 1970
Reprinted 1971, 1972, 1973, 1975, 1976, 1977, 1979,
1980, 1981, 1983, 1984, 1986

—

—

Made and printed in Great Britain by
Hazell Watson & Viney Limited,
Member of the BPCC Group,
Aylesbury, Bucks
Set in Intertype Plantin

Contents

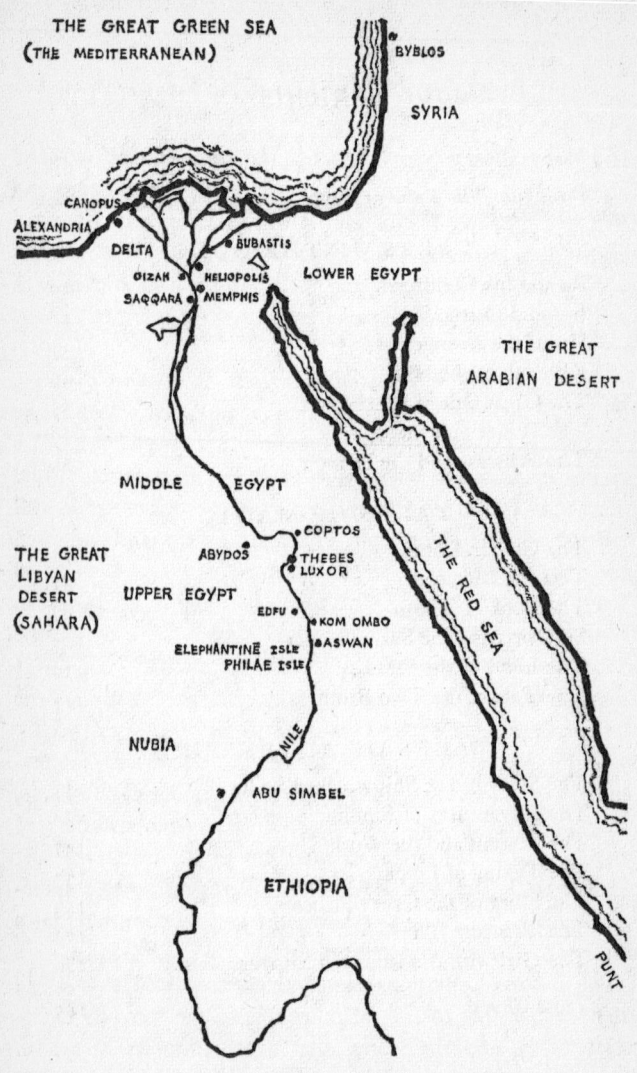

THE WORLD OF ANCIENT EGYPT

Prologue: The Land of Egypt

EGYPT has always been a land of mystery and magic – a land different from all others, difficult to understand, apart and alien, yet strangely fascinating. It was the most self-contained of all the countries of the ancient world; it lived its own life, practised its own religion and made up its own stories with hardly any outside influence either from or upon other civilizations.

When the ancient Greeks 'discovered' it in about 500 BC and began to write about it, Egyptian civilization was drawing towards the end of its three thousand years of existence. The first Greek historian whose works survive, Herodotus, visited it in about 450 BC and found that only the priests could still read the ancient hieroglyphs in which inscriptions had been carved or written on the monuments since the days when Menes, the first historical Pharaoh, united the 'Two Lands' in about 3200 BC. Yet the myths and the stories which the people were still telling had been handed down through all or many of those thirty centuries, and had hardly changed. After the time of Herodotus Ancient Egypt was preserved almost artificially by its Greek conquerors – Alexander the Great and the descendants of his general Ptolemy. It faded under the Romans, and was stamped out completely by the Arab invaders of AD 639–46. It has only been rediscovered during the last hundred and fifty years, when the hieroglyphs were interpreted, the ancient language translated and the tombs, temples and pyramids excavated and preserved.

The natural conditions in any land are often to a large extent responsible for its religious beliefs, the form its civilization takes, and the stories that evolve into its literature. The dead monotony of mud, with the plains of Mesopotamia stretching to the horizon in every direction, gave Babylon her dreary religion of hopeless despair; the breath-taking beauty of the mountains and valleys and gulfs of the sea in the glorious light of Greece produced the immortal myths and legends of that most lovely land; and the sharp, cold air and the nearness of bitter winter gave to our Norse ancestors the brilliant heroic fatalism of the sagas.

Egypt is the hardest land to imagine, even from its myths and stories, for those who have not seen it. 'Egypt is the gift of the Nile,' wrote the old Greek historian Hecataeus – and the Nile, indeed, *is* Egypt. Except for the fertile Delta in the north, a triangle of low-lying green land with sides each of roughly 150 miles, Egypt is the narrow valley of the Nile, a cleft in the desert running for many hundreds of miles – and a thousand more if we follow it up through the Sudan into Ethiopia.

'Going up the Nile is like running the gauntlet before Eternity,' wrote Rudyard Kipling fifty years ago on his first visit. 'Till one has seen it, one does not realize the amazing thinness of that little damp trickle of life that steals along undefeated through the jaws of established death. A rifle-shot would cover the widest limits of cultivation, a bow-shot would reach the narrower. . . . The weight of the Desert is on one, every day and every hour.'

Except in the Delta, if a man walked away from the river in either direction until he needed water, he would have died of thirst before he could walk back again for a drink. There are four thousand miles of desert to the west and nearly half that distance to the east (including the Red Sea).

Moreover, even in Egypt life depended on the annual Inundation – the rising of the Nile, due to heavy rain thousands of miles away in Abyssinia, which flooded both the valley and most of the Delta from June to October each year, and left a thick deposit of mud and silt in which the crops grew with amazing fertility – all kinds of corn and vegetables, and fruits such as grapes and melons and dates.

If the Inundation was too small, starvation faced Egypt, and many died of hunger if several 'lean years' came together at a time when the Pharaoh had had no Joseph to store grain in the good years against such a time of want.

With death always so near, the ancient Egyptians developed an obsession with death, yet not one that seems to have warped their lives. Egypt is a land of great, if peculiar beauty: the river shines in the intense sunlight, the groves of green date palms and tamarisks shelter for a while each year profusions of bright flowers; the cliffs at the edge of the desert – notably those behind Western Thebes – glow and shine and fade with indescribably lovely colours at sunrise and sunset; and in the sudden cold of darkness the stars shine with extraordinary brilliance in a sky like black velvet.

Ra, or, as he later became, Amen-Ra, the Sun-god was the first and most important of deities – and the River Nile itself came second, sometimes worshipped as Khnemu, but more usually as part of the whole principle of life and reproduction which came to be enshrined in the person of the goddess Isis.

But Osiris, god of the world of the dead, was the brother and husband of Isis and he was the greatest god of all – for all the dead would return to earth when he, the first human Pharaoh of Egypt, came back to be the eternal Pharaoh.

As Osiris had been a human Pharaoh who became a god, so each Pharaoh was held to be a god on earth who would become a god in heaven – in the Duat where Osiris reigned. So, from the earliest times, the tombs of the Pharaohs and the mortuary temples in which they were honoured were built of the most enduring stone that could be found, and covered with carvings, paintings and inscriptions which remain from so many thousands of years ago to tell us about their lives and beliefs, myths and stories. Houses, and palaces, were made of mud bricks for the short tenure of the living, and have nearly all disappeared; but the pyramids and the temples and the rock tombs were built to last for ever, and they are the oldest and still among the mightiest and most imposing of all ancient monuments.

The end of every story in Ancient Egypt, like the end of every life, was the stately funeral procession to the rock-hewn tomb at the edge of the desert on the western side of the Nile. There, after many ceremonies, the body was laid to rest in a safe place until the day when Osiris should return to earth and the spirits of the dead come back with him and abide once more in the bodies that had been their earthly homes – there to dwell for ever in his earthly kingdom of the undying.

Although all the Egyptians did their best to make fine tombs for themselves, and their children tried always to have their parents' bodies properly preserved and wrapped and laid in these tombs, it was naturally the Pharaohs who were honoured with the finest and most enduring dwelling places.

Those of the early Dynasties, such as Zoser and Khufu and Khafra, built the mighty pyramids for themselves which have survived to be their monuments for five thousand years. Later Pharaohs such as Hatshepsut and Rameses the Great and Seti I hollowed the vast rock tombs in the Valley of the Kings at Western Thebes – chamber beyond chamber going down into the rock for hundreds of feet.

In the heart of the pyramid or in the deepest rock chamber lay the body of the Pharaoh enclosed in a multitude of coffins, the innermost of gold and the outer of the hard granite stone of Syene, the modern Aswan. With him were laid treasures without number, and all his choicest possessions, from chariots and thrones to fans and boxes of sweet ointment; and there also were the Ushabti Figures – little models of men and women performing all the labours of this world, farming, fishing, weaving, cooking, rowing the Royal Boat, and so on: for in the life to come 'the good god Pharaoh' would live even as he had done upon earth, and must have all that had been his by right when he dwelt in Egypt.

On the walls of the tomb-chambers were painted and carved not only scenes from this world, but also from the next – so that he who dwelt in the tomb should know what to expect and what to do when he 'went West' into the Duat, the Land of the Dead.

How the ancient Egyptians knew so well what to expect during the journey through the Duat, no one seems quite to know. Doubtless there were stories of magicians and others who had travelled into that strange world and returned to tell of it – but all except one are lost to us, and the only survivor is very fragmentary, though the descriptions of the Duat and the Judgement before Osiris can be restored with the aid of the pictures and inscriptions from the tombs, and the rolls of papyrus called *The Book of the Dead* buried with those who could not afford to have the full instructions painted on the walls.

From the days when Menes became the first Pharaoh of a united Egypt, down almost to the time when Herodotus and other Greek travellers came as interested tourists, the ancient Egyptians lived their quiet and almost unchanging lives. There were some minor invasions from outside: once for a hundred years the Delta was held by mysterious invaders called the Hyksōs (who some scholars think may have been the Israelites); during the two hundred years before Herodotus paid his visit, Egypt was conquered for a time by the Assyrians, and then by the Persians. By the time of Rameses the Great (1290–1224 BC) Egypt held an empire over most of Palestine and Syria; but a century later the Greeks of the Mycenaean period were invading the Delta unsuccessfully.

However, ordinary life in Egypt changed little. The people lived simply, and usually fairly prosperously, tilling their fields after the Inundation; building the pyramids and temples and tombs during the four or five months of each year when the valley was under water and all agriculture ceased.

They had a fair amount of leisure: a good deal of it taken up with religious ceremonies, but time also for song and dance and music, and for telling stories. Usually these songs and tales were handed down by word of mouth and not written. Sometimes, if they concerned the gods – which also included the Pharaohs – they were carved in temples and shrines. Thus of the stories in this book *The Prince and the Sphinx* is preserved in hieroglyphs cut into a slab of stone in the tiny temple between the paws of the Great Sphinx at Giza; the story of *The Great Queen Hatshepsut* may be read on the walls of her temple (Der-el-Bahri) at Western Thebes; *The Princess and the Demon* on a sandstone tablet found in the Temple of Khonsu at Thebes and now in Paris, and *Khnemu of the Nile* is carved on the rocks at Elephantinē.

Ra and his Children, Horus the Avenger, and many of the descriptions in *The Land of the Dead* are pieced together from carvings and inscriptions in the Pyramid of Zoser, the tombs of Seti I and Rameses II and III, the Temple of Horus at Edfu, *The Book of the Dead* and other papyrus sources buried with those who could not afford to have this 'Guide to the Land of the Dead' carved or painted on the walls of their tombs.

Similar sources give fragments of the story of Osiris, but it so happens that the Greek historian and essayist Plutarch, who lived in the first century AD, told the whole legend in his treatise *Concerning Isis and Osiris* – the reliability of which is proved by the very early inscriptions at Abydos and elsewhere.

Most of the Tales of Magic and Adventure were written or written down during the last two thousand years of Ancient Egypt. *The Golden Lotus* and *Teta the Magician* come from the Westcar Papyrus now in Berlin, which is thought to have been written during the Twelfth Dynasty (2000–1785 BC).

The Tale of the Two Brothers was probably written by Ana, the favourite scribe of Pharaoh Seti II (about 1200 BC); *The Peasant and the Workman* appears in several defective papyri of uncertain date, which can be pieced together to make one complete version; *The Story of the Shipwrecked Sailor* is also very early and may even date from the Twelfth Dynasty, though experts differ about the age of the papyrus, which is now in Moscow.

Se-Osiris and the Sealed Letter, The Book of Thoth, The Adventures of Sinuhe and *The Taking of Joppa* are all from late manuscripts written after about 715 BC when 'Demotic' writing superseded the old hieroglyphs – but of course they are probably much older than the date at which the surviving copies were written and perhaps go back to the Nineteenth or Twentieth Dynasties, the period following the golden age of Rameses the Great.

The last three stories are preserved only in Greek versions. *The Story of the Greek Princess* was first told in Greek by Stesichorus (*c.* 600 BC) of whose works only fragments remain; it is given several chapters by Herodotus, and was used as the basis for a play by Euripides: but the basic story was obviously Egyptian, for the Greeks could not understand at all about the Princess's *Ka* or 'Double', which appears nowhere else in Greek myth or legend. This Egyptian origin was clearly recognized by Rider Haggard and Andrew Lang who made use of some of the story in their fine romance of the days of Merneptah, son of Rameses the Great, *The World's Desire*: and Haggard made better use still of the *Ka* in his *Morning Star* which is one of the best re-creations of Ancient Egypt ever written.

The Treasure Thief was told to Herodotus during his visit to Egypt, and he included it in his *History*. As for *The Girl with the Rose-red Slippers*, the earliest version of the Cinderella story, Herodotus certainly knew of Rhodopis, who was almost his contemporary, though he confused her with an earlier adventuress-queen; but the full tale was given by another Greek, Aelian, in his *Varia Historia* in the third century AD.

And so these tales of Ancient Egypt represent a written literature of over two thousand years, stretching back to more than four thousand years ago, and perhaps as much as five thousand if we assume that the tales of the gods were handed down by word of mouth from the days of the first Pharaohs until Zoser and his successors began to carve them in hieroglyphs on the walls of tomb-chambers and temples. The best of the relatively few that remain out of that distant age have been collected here and retold: the oldest stories in the world, yet most of them stories that never grow old in themselves, though their dress may have the charm of age and distance: stories that catch for us an echo out of that incredibly distant past, that bring us bright, tantalizing glimpses from the lost world of Ancient Egypt:

> The murmur of the fallen creeds
> Like winds among the wind-shaken reeds
> Along the banks of holy Nile.

Tales of the Gods

Ra and his Children

BEFORE the land of Egypt rose out of the waters at the beginning of the world, Ra the Shining One came into being. He was all-powerful, and the secret of his power lay in his Name which was hidden from all the world. Having this power, he had only to name a thing, and that thing too came into being.

'I am Khepera at the dawn, and Ra at noon, and Tum in the evening,' he said – and as he said it, behold, he was the sun rising in the east, passing across the sky and setting in the west. And this was the first day of the world.

When he named Shu, the wind blew. The rain fell when he named Tefnut the spitter. After this he spoke the name of Geb, and the earth rose above the waters of the sea. He cried, 'Nut!' – and that goddess was the arch of the sky stretching over the earth with her feet on one horizon and her hands on the other. Then he named Hapi, and the sacred River Nile flowed through Egypt to make it fruitful.

Then Ra went on to name all the things on earth, which grew into being at his words. Last of all he spoke the words for 'Man' and 'Woman', and soon there were people dwelling throughout the land of Egypt.

After this Ra himself took on the shape of a man and became the first Pharaoh of Egypt. For thousands of years he reigned over the land, and there was peace and plenty. The Nile rose each year and flooded the fields; then it sank back into its channel, leaving the rich coating of mud which made sure of fine crops as the cool spring turned into the baking summer. There were no lean years when the Nile did not rise high enough; nor were there any years when the floods rose too high or lasted too long. It was the golden age of the world, and ever afterwards the Egyptians spoke of the good things 'which happened in the time of Ra'.

At last, however, even Ra grew old: for it was decreed that no man should live for ever, and he had made himself a man to rule over Egypt. And when he was old and his bones were like silver, his flesh like gold and his hair like lapis lazuli, he could no longer rule well over the people of Egypt, nor fight against Apophis, the Dragon of Evil who had grown out of the evil vapours in the darkness of the night and sought ever to devour all that was good and bright and kissed by the sun.

Presently the evil of Apophis entered into the souls of the people of Egypt and many of them rebelled against Ra and did evil in his sight, worshipping the Dragon of Darkness instead of the Eye of Day.

Ra perceived these things and the plots which the evil

among men were preparing against his divine majesty. Then he spoke to his attendants, saying, 'Gather together the high gods who are my court. Summon Shu and Tefnut, bid Geb and Nut hasten to the council hall – send even for Nun, the spirit of the waters out of which I arose at the beginning of the world. Gather them secretly: let not the evil among men know that I am aware of their doings.'

Then the gods came into the presence of Ra, bowing in turn before him and kissing the ground at his feet in token of loyalty.

When all were gathered Nun spoke for them, saying, 'Life, health, strength be to you, Ra, Pharaoh of Egypt, maker of all things! Speak to us so that we may hear your divine will.'

Then Ra answered, 'Nun, eldest of all things, and all ye gods whom I have called into being – look upon mankind, whom also I made at a glance of my all-seeing Eye, naming them in the beginning that they might appear upon the earth and multiply to be my servants in life and in death. See, they have plotted against me, they have done evil things – the wicked among them gather even now in Upper Egypt to work further ill in my sight. Tell me, shall I slay them all with a burning glance of my Eye?'

Nun answered, speaking for all the gods: 'Ra, greater than I out of whom you came in the beginning; you who are mightier than all the gods you have created – if you send forth the burning glance of your Eye to slay mankind, it will turn all the land of Egypt into a desert. Therefore make a power that will smite men and women only; send out that which will burn the evil but not harm the good.'

Then answered Ra, 'I will not send forth the burning glance of my Eye. Instead I will send Sekhmet against mankind!'

As he spoke the name, Sekhmet leapt into being, in form as a mighty lioness of gigantic size. Away she sped into Upper Egypt, and slaughtered and devoured mankind until the Nile ran red with blood and the earth beside it became a great red marsh.

Before long the most wicked among men had been slain by Sekhmet, and the rest prayed to Ra for mercy. And Ra wished to spare them, for he had no desire to slay all of mankind and leave himself the ruler of a desolate earth with no human beings to serve him.

But, having tasted blood, Sekhmet would not cease from her hunting. Day by day she stalked through the land of Egypt slaying all whom she met; and night by night she hid herself among the rocks on the edge of the desert, waiting for the sun to rise so that she might hunt once more.

Then said Ra, 'Sekhmet cannot be stayed except by a trick. If I can deceive her and save mankind from her sharp teeth and from her claws, I will give her greater power yet over them so that her heart shall rejoice and she shall not feel that honour has been taken from her.'

So Ra summoned before him swift and speedy messengers and commanded them, saying, 'Run like the shadow of a body – swifter and more silently than the body itself – to the island of Elephantinē that lies in the Nile below the First Cataract. Bring me the red ochre that is found there alone – bring it with speed.'

Away sped the messengers through the darkness and returned to Heliopolis, the city of Ra, bearing loads of the red ochre of Elephantinē. There, by Ra's command, all the priestesses of the Temple of the Sun, and all the maidservants of the royal court were set to crushing barley and making beer. Seven thousand jars did they make and, by the command of Ra, they mingled the red ochre of Elephantinē with it so that it gleamed in the moonlight red as blood.

'Now,' said Ra, 'carry this upstream to protect mankind. Carry it to where Sekhmet means to slaughter men when day returns, and pour it out upon the earth as a trap for her.'

Day dawned and Sekhmet came out into the sunlight from her lair among the rocks and looked about her, seeking whom she might devour. She saw no living thing. But, in the place where yesterday she had slain many men, she saw that the fields were covered to the depth of three hands' breadths with what seemed to be blood.

Sekhmet saw and laughed with a laugh like the roar of a hungry lioness. Thinking that it was the blood she had shed upon the previous day, she stooped and drank greedily. Again and again she drank, until the strength of the beer mounted to her brain and she could neither hunt nor kill.

As the day drew to its close she came reeling down to Heliopolis where Ra awaited her – and when the sun touched the horizon she had not slain a single man or woman since the evening before.

'You come in peace, sweet one,' said Ra, 'peace be with you and a new name. No longer are you Sekhmet the Slayer: you are Hathor the Lady of Love. Yet your power over mankind shall be greater even than it was – for the passion of love shall be stronger than the passion of hate, and all shall know love, and all shall be your victims. Moreover, in memory of this day, the priestesses of love shall drink the beer of Heliopolis made red with the ochre of Elephantinē on the first day of each year at a great festival in honour of Hathor.'

So mankind was saved by Ra, and given both a new delight and a new pain.

Isis and Osiris

WHILE Ra yet reigned upon earth as the first Pharaoh of Egypt, Thoth, the god of wisdom and magic whom he had created at the beginning of the world, uttered a prophecy.

'If Nut, the Lady of the Heavens, bears a son, he will one day rule in Egypt.'

'Nut shall never bear a son, nor any children at all!' said Ra angrily. 'No child of Nut shall take my throne from me! Lo, now I lay this curse upon her: she shall give birth to no child on any day in any year – no, nor in the night time either. I have spoken, and what I have decreed cannot be altered.'

Nut was heart-broken at this. Yet Thoth had said that her son should rule in Egypt, and he was the wisest of all the gods. So she went to Thoth, who loved her, and begged for his aid.

'Grant me your love, and I will show you how your wish may be fulfilled – and yet Ra's curse remain unbroken,' said Thoth.

Nut consented readily to this, and Thoth soon devised a clever scheme. He visited Khonsu the Moon-god and challenged him to a game of draughts. Khonsu was a great gambler, and very soon the stakes were high indeed – but highest of all on the Moon's side, for he was wagering his own light. And he had no chance of beating clever Thoth, who went on playing – and winning – until he had won enough of the Moon's light from Khonsu to make five extra days. These days he fitted in between the end of the old year and the beginning of the new. Before this there had only been three hundred and sixty days in each year: that number remained the same, but the five days between each year set the calendar right. Moreover, since that great game of draughts the Moon has not had enough light to shine at the full throughout each month, but dwindles down into darkness and then comes slowly to his full glory again.

Here, now, were five days that were not any days in any year – and on these days Nut's five children were born: Osiris upon the first day, Harmachis upon the second day, Set upon the third, Isis on the fourth and Nephthys on the fifth.

When Osiris was born there were many signs and wonders. A great voice from heaven was heard crying, 'The Lord of All comes forth into the light!' A woman drawing water at the well was suddenly seized with the spirit of prophecy and cried aloud, 'Osiris the King is born.' And in Thebes a certain man called Pamyles heard a voice coming from the temple of Ra which bade him proclaim the birth of Egypt's greatest king, Osiris the saviour of mankind.

By the advice of Thoth, Nut entrusted the baby Osiris to Pamyles to bring up: but Thoth himself instructed both Osiris and Isis in all the wisdom of the gods and in the hidden lore of which he was the master.

Isis learnt so quickly, and also persuaded Khonsu to teach her all the mysteries of the Moon, that she became the greatest magician that Egypt has ever known.

When they were grown up, Isis and Osiris married, and Nephthys married Set; and following their example, the human Pharaohs of Egypt ever afterwards married their own sisters. Though most of them had many other wives as well, the sister-bride was always the Queen.

Isis was not yet Queen, however, nor Osiris King. For Ra still ruled on earth as the Pharaoh of Egypt, though in his human form he grew older and older, his head shook with the palsy of extreme old age, and he dribbled at the mouth.

Wise Isis pondered in her heart how she might end the reign of Ra upon earth so that Osiris could become King. The wisdom which Thoth had taught her told her that only by learning Ra's hidden Name could she gain power over him;

the witchcraft of the Moon which Khonsu had shown her suggested a dark scheme to her heart.

All living things were made by Ra, and without him no new creature could be created. Yet Isis made the first cobra – the 'uraeus' which became the sacred serpent of Egypt. As Ra passed on his way each morning to visit the Upper and the Lower Lands of Egypt, he dribbled at the mouth and his spittle fell in the dust by the roadside. Isis gathered the moist clay so made and fashioned it into the likeness of a hooded snake; she set in it the fiery poison of midnight magic, and she hid it in the grass beside the way which Ra was accustomed to take.

Next day as he stepped out to view his kingdom the glorious light of Ra's Eye fell upon the cobra that Isis had fashioned, and gave it life. The cobra reared its head out of the grass, bit Ra in the heel, and slipped away out of sight.

For a little while Ra was speechless with surprise. Then, as pain shot through him like fire, he uttered a great cry which rang through all the land of Egypt.

At once all the gods and goddesses came hastening to him, Isis among them, and bowed down before him and asked, 'What is it that troubles you, Maker of Gods and Men?'

'Something has wounded me!' cried Ra. 'Yet my heart does not know it, my eyes have not seen it, my hand did not make it, I do not recognize it among the things I have made – I who made all things. Therefore let the children of the gods be brought before me, those who know magic spells, those whose wisdom reaches to heaven, for it may be that one of them can help me.'

So, one by one, the gods and their children came before Ra. But none of them could help him, and ever the pain of the cobra's bite grew fiercer and fiercer.

At last it was the turn of Isis. She knelt humbly before Ra and said, 'What is it, divine father, that has stabbed you? Is it some snake from amongst those you made that has lifted up its head against you? If so, I shall cast it down with powerful magic: I shall make it hide its head from the sight of your divine eyes.'

Then said Ra: 'As I went on my way, as I walked between the Two Lands of Egypt to look upon all I have created, I was bitten by a snake that I did not see – by a serpent that I did not make – with a poison that I do not know. It is not fire, neither is it water: yet one moment I am colder than water, and the next moment I am hotter than fire. Now my body is sweating, and now it is shivering. My eyes are clouded and I cannot see; my head burns as with the fierce beams of midsummer.'

Isis bowed her head before Ra and spoke softly: 'Divine father, I can cure this grievous poison. Tell me your Secret Name – for you can only be cured if that Name is mingled with my spells.'

Then Ra spoke in turn the many names by which he was worshipped – the names that told of all that he had made – the heavens and the earth, the sea and the mysteries of the two horizons, darkness and light, the great river Nile, all living creatures and all else besides.

'Yes,' he ended, 'I am Khepera in the dawning, I am Ra at noon, I am Tum when the shadows of evening fall over the earth.'

But the poison was not checked in its course as Isis spoke one name after another, and she said again, 'Divine father, your Secret Name is not among those you have told me. Tell me that Name and the poison will come forth – he whose Name of Power is spoken in my charm shall live.'

The poison burned fiercer yet: it was more powerful than the hottest flame of fire, and Ra cried out, 'Swear first that none ever shall know my Secret Name save only Horus, the son you will bear to Osiris – Horus who shall rule Egypt when Osiris has passed westward to the Land of the Dead.'

Isis swore the oath, and the Secret Name passed from Ra's heart into hers: his *Ka* or double whispering it to her *Ka*. The Name she learnt was not 'Amen', nor has it ever been known: but the name 'Amen' seems to have been as it were, the body of that Name of which the hidden part was the *Ka* – for it was as Amen-Ra that the greatest of the gods came to be worshipped for thousands of years afterwards in Ancient Egypt.

Once she knew the Secret Name, Isis mingled the knowledge with her spell and chanted: 'Flow forth, poison of the cobra! Flow forth from Amen-Ra! Come from the burning god at my spell – for he has shown me his Hidden Name: Ra is living and the poison is dead, through the spells of Isis the Mistress of the Gods – she who alone knows Amen-Ra by his own Name.'

Then the pain of the serpent's poison faded away and Ra

felt it no more. But nevertheless he ceased to reign as a king upon earth and took his place in the heavens where, day by day, he crossed over from the east to the west in the likeness of the Sun itself, and night by night he passed under the earth through the twelve regions called the Duat which the spirits of the dead also must pass if they would win to Ra's eternal kingdom.

As soon as Ra had taken his place in the heavens, Osiris became Pharaoh of Egypt with Isis as his Queen. They built the great city of Thebes as their capital, and ruled well and wisely.

When Osiris came to the throne the Egyptians were cannibals, and lived more like wild animals than human beings. All this he and Isis altered very soon, teaching mankind to sow and reap both wheat and barley to make bread; how to grow various fruits such as the date and the grape for food and wine; how to make laws and live in peace under them; and how to do due honour to the gods and build temples for them – the first and greatest being that of Amen-Ra at Thebes.

As soon as the land of the Delta and Upper Egypt as far as Thebes had learnt all the arts of peace and civilization, Osiris left Isis to rule over it and set out to teach the men and women in more distant parts. He took no army with him, but only a band of priests and musicians, and even the wildest tribes harkened to his kindly words and were won over by the sweet strains of music.

Not all men, even in Egypt, followed Osiris, however. There was evil awake in the world to strive against good – and in Egypt that evil found its leader in Set, the younger brother of Osiris and Isis.

Set would have rebelled and seized the throne while Osiris was away from Egypt on his mission. But Isis kept such good watch that he knew he would have no success. So he pretended to be a faithful subject and loving brother of Pharaoh and his

Queen. But he gathered secretly to him seventy-two wicked men, all of whom were ready to join in a conspiracy against Osiris, and to them he added Aso the queen of Ethiopia who was on a visit to the court of Thebes.

As soon as Osiris returned, Set invited him to a great feast which he had prepared in honour of his brother.

Suspecting nothing, Osiris came unattended, and was welcomed by Set and his seventy-two companions.

It was a very splendid feast during which each of the guests vied with the others to do honour to Osiris. At last, as it was drawing to a close, Set said, 'We have all paid our tributes of praise to my beloved brother, the good god Pharaoh Osiris. Now, to end the feast, I have a gift for one of my guests – but this time I do not know who it will be!'

Set clapped his hands and his servants brought into the hall a most beautiful chest made of cedar wood from Lebanon and ebony from Ethiopia, inlaid with gold and silver, with ivory and lapis lazuli, and with precious stones.

When it was placed in the midst of the guests, the servants retired, the doors of the hall were shut, and Set spoke again.

'Here is my gift to one of my guests. It shall be his who fits most perfectly into the chest!'

All were admiring its beauty with cries of delight; and now they began one by one to see how well each of them fitted into it. But some were too tall and some were too short, some too fat and others too thin.

'Let me try,' said Osiris at last. He stepped into the chest and lay down – and it fitted him perfectly, for Set had secretly obtained the exact measurements of his brother's body.

'It is mine!' cried Osiris gaily. 'See, it fits me like the skin I was born in!'

'It is certainly yours,' answered Set. 'And it is fit to be the coffin you shall die in!'

So saying he slammed down the lid, and with feverish haste

he and his evil companions nailed it up tightly, filled every crack with molten lead, and cast it secretly into the Nile.

It was the time of the Inundation, and the swift waters hurried it out through the Delta and into the sea near the city of Tanis. Away it went over the waves until it came at last to the city of Byblos in Syria, the oldest city in the world. There a great wave lifted it over the shingle and cast it into the heart of a young tamarisk tree growing near the shore. Speedily the tamarisk clasped it with its branches and grew round it until the chest was completely hidden in its trunk.

Of all trees this tamarisk was the fairest, with lovely blossoms and sweetly-scented wood. Very soon it became famous throughout Syria – more famous even than the great cedars on Mount Lebanon at the foot of which stood the city of Byblos. Presently the fame of the tree brought Malcander the king of that land to see it, with his wife Queen Astartē; and it seemed to them so wonderful that Malcander had it cut down and a pillar fashioned out of its trunk which he set up in the place of honour in his palace. And all men marvelled at the beauty of the wood and its fragrance, though none knew that it held the body of a god.

Meanwhile Isis learnt what had happened, and set out at once in search of the body of Osiris. For until the proper funeral rites were performed his spirit could not be free to enter the Duat, the Land of the Dead.

But first of all she went to the island of Chemmis in one of the streams of the Nile Delta; and there, tended by Buto the kindly goddess of Lower Egypt, her son Horus was born.

When she could travel, Isis set out once more in search of the body of her husband. But she left Horus in the care of Buto, and as a further safeguard against Set she loosened the island of Chemmis from its foundations and set it afloat – sometimes on the Nile, sometimes on the sea itself – so that Set might not find it.

Then she cut her hair in token of mourning and went hither and thither on her search throughout Egypt. At first she had no success; but presently she found a group of children who had seen the beautifully decorated chest floating down the Nile near Tanis and heading for the Great Green Sea.

Asking the children at their games along the sea-shore, Isis followed the chest until she came at last to Byblos. And only then was her magic able to show her where the body of Osiris was.

Isis sat by the shore at Byblos in the likeness of an old woman. When Queen Astartë's serving-maids came down to the sea to wash their clothes and bathe in the waves, Isis spoke kindly to them and taught them how to braid their hair – for no one before this had ever thought to twist their hair into plaits and twine it on their heads with flowers and leaves as ornaments.

When they returned to the palace Astartë asked her maids where they had learnt this new art, and they told her of the dignified old woman who sat on a rock beside the sea.

Full of curiosity, Astartë bade them bring her to the palace. When Isis came, Astartë realized that here was a stranger of no ordinary kind, though she thought her no more than a woman filled with the wisdom for which Egypt was already famous. So she welcomed her, and begged her to dwell in the palace and tend her little son the Prince Diktys – a delicate baby who seemed likely to die.

Isis nursed Diktys so well that day by day he grew and became stronger in a way that seemed more than natural. Queen Astartë was curious, the more so because her maids told her that each night the strange nurse would turn them out of the room and lock the door. Then they would hear her heap up the fire; and after that there was a long silence broken only by a sound like the twittering of a swallow.

So Astartē hid herself in the room one night. Presently she saw Isis turn out the serving-maids, bar the door and heap up the fire. When the fire was burning fiercely, Isis made a glowing red space between the logs, took the baby Diktys and placed him in it. And immediately she herself turned into a swallow and flew round and round the pillar which held the body of Osiris, twittering mournfully.

With a scream Astartē rushed forward and snatched Diktys out of the fire – to find that he was quite unharmed by it, and indeed began to cry indignantly at being plucked so suddenly from such a warm and comfortable bed.

Full of fear, Astartē turned to flee, clutching her child in her arms. But instead she sank to the floor and hid her eyes: for Isis stood before her, tall and beautiful and quite obviously a goddess.

'Foolish woman!' cried Isis. 'Had you but left your son to my care I would have burned away all that was human in him and made him one of the gods, even as I am. But now he will die when old age comes to him, as all men do – if indeed death does not come to him sooner.'

Again and again King Malcander and Queen Astartē knelt before Isis, begging her to forgive them and offering all the riches of Byblos if she would continue to tend their son.

'That I cannot do,' said Isis. 'But I will leave my blessing on you if you will give me what yonder pillar contains.'

Then the King sent for his workmen, and the pillar was taken down and split open. Inside rested the coffin of Osiris; and when this had been lifted out Isis poured perfume on the pillar, and said, 'Place this in your most sacred temple, and it will bring pilgrims to Byblos for many ages. For this wood has held the body of a god.'

So the people of Byblos built a temple in which they set the wooden pillar; and it became known as the Temple of Baalat

Gebal, 'The Lady of Byblos', the remains of which may be seen to this day.

But Isis set the coffin on a boat and sailed away from Byblos. When she was passing the mouth of the river Phaedros, the current flowed so strongly that it seemed about to drive the ship out to sea – so Isis in a moment of anger cast a spell upon the river and dried up the water.

When the ship was sailing gently over the sea once more in the direction of Egypt, Isis bade all leave her by herself, went into the cabin and opened the coffin. But the prince of Byblos who commanded her escort, Maneros, was so filled with curiosity that he hid in the cabin and peeped over her shoulder at what was in the coffin. Isis felt his presence and turning gave him one glance – one awful look of anger – and he fell dead to the floor.

When the ship reached Egypt, Isis guided it to where the floating island of Chemmis was waiting for her and bade the sailors set the coffin on its shore. As soon as this was done and she stood beside it, she bade the sailors row home to Byblos as fast as they could, and she sent a wind to help them on their way.

But she herself floated up the Nile on the island, where Buto was still guarding the infant Horus, and hid it among the reeds of the Delta until she could perform the funeral rites of Osiris.

However, her quest was by no means at an end. For on the very next night Set and his followers came hunting through the darkness and the moonlight – for Set best loved the hours of darkness when evil things wander the earth.

As ill luck would have it, he came to the island of Chemmis that seemed now to be part of the firm earth. Isis hid with Horus deep down among the reeds and escaped his notice. But he saw the chest which had become the coffin of Osiris, and at once he recognized it.

With a great howl of rage and hate he snatched the body of his murdered brother out of the chest, tore it into fourteen pieces, and scattered them far and wide over the land of Egypt.

'It seems hard to destroy the body of a god!' he cried. 'Yet now I have destroyed Osiris and kept his spirit out of the Duat!'

He went on his way laughing. But Isis crept out of her hiding-place, entrusted Horus once more to Buto, and set out again in search of the pieces of her husband's body.

As she rowed hither and thither on the Nile in her boat made of papyrus, the very crocodiles took pity on her and let her pass – and ever since anyone sailing on the Nile in a papyrus boat has been safe from the crocodiles, who think that it is still Isis searching for the last piece of the body of Osiris.

For she found all but one piece, which had fallen into the Nile and been eaten by certain fishes who were accursed for ever after. But the other pieces she found with the help of Anubis, the son of Set and Nephthys, who took the shape of a wild dog in order to help her the better in her search.

Fearing lest Set should desecrate even the tomb of Osiris, Isis buried him in the thirteen different places at which she found the pieces of his body, making a complete body by her magic in each place so that a great funeral might be performed. And for this reason thirteen cities of Egypt all boasted that they held the burial place of Osiris.

Yet some say that in her fear of Set, Isis deceived even the high priests and people of the thirteen cities by burying the whole body of Osiris (adding the one missing piece by magic) on the holy island of Philae beyond the First Cataract above Elephantinē. And they prove this by the fact that in later years the most sacred oath an Egyptian could swear was 'By Him who sleeps at Philae!'

Whatever his earthly burial, once it was accomplished, the

spirit of Osiris passed into the Duat. There he became the King of the Dead, welcoming all those whom the Judges of the Dead found worthy to enter his kingdom, and adding them to his army of the blessed with whom he would return to reign on earth after the last great battle with Set.

Horus the Avenger

WHEN the body of Osiris was safely buried and his spirit had gone to dwell in the Duat, Isis hastened back to the floating island of Chemmis to guard the baby Horus. For Set now ruled in Egypt, and above all things he desired to slay Horus as he had slain his father Osiris.

Isis well knew the danger which threatened Horus, and yet at first she seemed powerless to protect him. For, though she guarded the baby both day and night, Set found where he was hidden and made his way onto the island when it had come to rest against the west bank of the Nile.

When night fell, Set took the shape of a scorpion and crept up to the cradle in which Horus lay sleeping in a simple hut among the high papyrus reeds. When the moon rose, Isis stepped out of the hut to make her prayer to Khonsu the Moon-god that he would guard her son.

While she prayed, the scorpion who was Set crept into the cradle and stung Horus. Hearing the baby scream, Isis rushed back into the hut and snatched him up in her arms while Set slipped away into the darkness unseen, and left the island of Chemmis long before it floated away from the shore next morning.

All night Isis tried every spell she knew to cure Horus of the scorpion's poison. But all was in vain, and when the sun rose the child lay lifeless in her arms.

Then in her despair Isis cried aloud to Thoth for help, and swiftly the thrice-mighty, the all-wise god stood before her.

'See!' she wailed. 'Set has slain the son even as he slew the father! Yet Horus was born to be the Avenger of Osiris: say, wise Thoth, how this can be?'

Then Thoth answered, 'Horus shall live again. His spirit

has but left him for a while to visit the spirit of Osiris in the Duat. It shall return in the shape of the Bennu bird – and in days to come the Bennu shall die in the bright heat of Ra's glance as it perches on the great obelisk at Heliopolis, and out of its ashes shall the new Bennu rise, and his fame shall be known throughout the world.* But before Horus returns to earth and while his spirit dwells safely in the Duat with Osiris, I will call a council of the gods to decide who shall rule in Egypt.'

The council of the gods was held at Heliopolis on the eastern bank of the Nile at the place where the river divides into the many streams of the Delta – the spot which divides Upper and Lower Egypt.

When all were assembled before Amen-Ra, the Father of Gods and Men, Set put his case, saying that as the brother of Osiris, he should be the next Pharaoh – 'And I am already the ruler of Egypt,' he ended fiercely, 'for my followers hold all the land, and if anyone tries to take it from me, I shall lay it waste with fire and water.'

But wise Thoth spoke for Horus, saying, 'Even as Osiris the first-born was the true King of Egypt, so his first-born son Horus should be the king who succeeds him.'

'You would not have a babe to rule Egypt!' cried Set. 'And what proof have we that this child Horus, if still alive, is indeed the son of Osiris – for Osiris died long before he was born!'

Then Isis sprang forward and spoke so well and so persuasively that Set saw that the gods were certain to be won by her words.

'So you would let Egypt be ruled by a woman!' he shouted suddenly. 'Send Isis away, let her not take part in this council – she pleads for her son only so that she herself can rule all things! Remember how she won the land of Egypt for her

* Thoth's prophecy was fulfilled – for the Bennu bird of Heliopolis was called the Phoenix by the Greeks.

husband when she learnt the Secret Name of Ra! Send her away, or I will bring war even among the gods and kill you who stand here one by one until all dwell with Osiris in the Duat.'

When Set had spoken Ra broke up the council for that day, saying, 'In the morning we will meet once more to decide this matter. Let our place of meeting be upon the Central Island here, where the Nile divides – and let the ferryman take good heed that Isis does not come across the river to it.'

So the gods and goddesses passed on to the island. But Isis, having taken counsel with Thoth, sought out her sister Nephthys, the wife of Set who had deserted her husband after the murder of Osiris and joined Isis, bringing her son Anubis with her.

Nephthys had not been at the council of the gods, for she dreaded lest they should compel her to return to her husband Set, whom she now hated and feared. She agreed willingly to help Isis in her plot against Set, disguised herself as her sister and lent Isis the head-dress shaped like a basket which she herself was accustomed to wear.

With the aid of her magic, Isis made herself look like Nephthys in face and voice as well as in her garments. Then, as soon as the full moon was shining over the river, she went down to the water's edge, and bade the ferryman take her over to the island.

At first he feared to do so thinking that her presence might anger Ra and Set almost as much as her sister's. But Isis spoke to him with gentle words and offered him a rich gift.

'My sister is forbidden to sit in the council of the gods,' she said, 'but I, Nephthys, have not been denied my rights, and I come to speak on behalf of Horus the son of Isis and Osiris.'

So the ferryman rowed her across to the island, never suspecting that she was other than she seemed. And when she found Set, he also was deceived and exclaimed, 'Nephthys, my Queen! I would have sent messengers to seek and bring you back to me on the morrow when I have been proclaimed Pharaoh of Egypt by all the gods in council. I am glad that you have returned to me of your own free will.'

'How could I stay away from you when I was free to come?' murmured Isis in the voice of Nephthys. 'Ah, my dear lord, did you not know that I had been kept away by the wicked magic of my sister Isis?'

Now Set knew very well that Nephthys had left him by her own wish, and he had small faith in her excuses. But as she stood there in the moonlight, so slim and beautiful, with her lovely eyes shining with love, Set forgot all his cunning and wished only to have Nephthys as his wife once more.

'Come back to me indeed,' he said, 'and I will forgive you all that is past, and make you my Queen.'

'First,' said the supposed Nephthys, 'you must swear an oath before all the gods in council that my son shall be Pharaoh of Egypt as soon as the time comes for him to rule this land – and that you will do him no harm nor plot anything against him unless he himself should attack you.'

'Yes, yes, I'll promise that Anubis shall succeed me as Pharaoh,' exclaimed Set impatiently, moving to embrace her.

'You must not touch me,' she said, drawing back, 'until you have sworn the oath.'

Nor would she let Set embrace her, though she sat by his side until the dawn came, drinking the rich red wine of the Delta – or seeing that he drank it – and singing him sweet love-songs.

In the morning she let him take her arm to support his drunken steps to the place on the island where the council of the gods was to be held. And at her prompting he swore to her before them all this oath:

'I swear by Him who sleeps at Philae that your son shall be Pharaoh of Egypt as soon as the time comes for him to rule this land, and that I will do him no harm nor plot anything against him unless he himself should attack me or try to take my throne.'

As soon as the oath was sworn, Isis laughed with the sweet, silvery laugh like the tinkling of the bells on the sistrum which she usually carried. And as she laughed, her face changed with her voice, she took off the head-dress of Nephthys, and all could see that it was indeed Isis to whom the drunken Set had sworn his oath.

'What further need the gods in council to declare, except that Set must keep the oath which he has sworn by Him who sleeps at Philae?' she cried. 'I am Isis, and he has sworn that my son, my only son, Horus, is the rightful Pharaoh of Egypt!'

Then all the gods laughed at the trick Isis had played, and

even Ra's brow grew bright – for since Set had sworn, there was no more to be said. And all the gods knew in their hearts that Horus was the rightful king.

But Set bellowed with rage like a mad hippopotamus, and cried in a voice which shook the hills like thunder: 'Not so easily shall Horus win my kingdom! When he is grown, let him come against me, and I will slay him and feast on his flesh, and become King indeed!'

Then he went away into the deserts of the south above the First Cataract with all his followers, and there was peace in Egypt for a while.

But all knew that the great war was to come. And, whether in the Duat or after his spirit returned to his body on the island of Chemmis, Horus was being trained every day to be the Avenger of Osiris.

Many times Osiris himself came from the Duat to instruct his son. And one day he said to Horus, 'Tell me, my son, what is the noblest thing a man can do?'

'Avenge his father and his mother for the evil done to them,' answered Horus.

'And what creature do you think most useful to take into battle with you?'

'A horse,' was the prompt answer.

'Would not a lion be of greater assistance?' asked Osiris.

'It would if a man *needed* assistance,' replied Horus. 'But a horse would be far more useful for cutting off an enemy's flight and slaying him.'

'Now, my son,' said Osiris solemnly, 'I perceive that your training is complete and the time has come for you to lead your followers into battle against Set.'

Then Osiris returned into the Duat, for in the living world he could not yet fight against Set. But Horus armed himself for the battle, gathered together his followers, and sought the aid of Harmachis, the god of the rising sun, the brother of

Osiris and Set, who so far had played no part in the struggle for the rule of Egypt.

But Set was watching all that Horus did, and he knew that the time had come when his oath to Isis bound him no longer. So he took upon himself the shape of a black pig – black as a thunder-cloud, fierce to look at, with tusks to strike terror into the bravest heart. He hid himself in the reeds where the island of Chemmis had come to rest in the Delta, near where in after days the city of Buto was to arise in honour of the goddess who had protected the infant Horus.

Harmachis and Horus met there alone together to make their plans, and Harmachis said: 'Let me speak a great spell and gaze into your eyes that are as bright as the midday sun. There I may see all that Set is planning against us, and where his followers lie in wait to attack us.'

So he spoke the spells and the eyes of Horus began to shine like the sun at noontide, and Harmachis of the rising sun gazed into them. At first they were like the Great Green Sea, clouded like lapis lazuli; but soon they began to grow clear like glass, and Harmachis knew that in a moment he would see through them to the very ends of the earth.

But suddenly the great black pig charged squealing out of the reeds.

'Beware of the black pig!' cried Harmachis. 'Never have I seen one so big or fierce!'

Horus turned and looked: for the two gods were off their guard and neither realized that it was no ordinary pig but Set the Evil, and they were not prepared against his magic.

Then Set aimed a blow of fire like a lightning flash at the eyes of Horus. And Horus covered his eyes with his hands crying, 'It is Set! And he has smitten me in the eyes with fire!'

But when Harmachis turned, Set the black pig had gone, and he could do no more than utter a curse which rested upon all pigs ever after and on all who touched them – save only on the night of the full Moon when black pigs were sacrificed to Horus.

Meanwhile the eyes of Horus were darkened for a little while as the sun is darkened when the thunderclouds speed over the Delta in the time of rain. But soon they grew bright once more and he set out in the boat of Harmachis up the Nile to the land of Upper Egypt where the sky is always blue.

On the way they fought several battles with the forces of Set, the evil men who worshipped him and did not follow the teachings of the good god Osiris. Their first outpost was near Memphis where the Delta ends. Here Horus turned himself into a great winged disc that glowed like a ball of fire, with wings on either side like the colours of the sky at sunset.

'Your eyes shall not see, and your minds shall be darkened likewise!' he cried. And at once as each man looked at his neighbour, he saw a stranger; and when any of them spoke, he seemed to hear a foreign tongue.

Then the first army of Set cried out, 'The enemy has come amongst us in disguise!' and they fell upon each other and slew and slew until none were left alive.

Horus flew back to Harmachis, and when he had taken on his own shape once more, Harmachis embraced him and gave him a draught of wine mixed with water – and in remembrance of that battle libations of wine and water were poured to Horus ever after.

Up the river sailed the boat of Harmachis, and presently the next wave of the enemy came against them, wearing the forms of crocodiles and hippopotami – ready to attack both on the banks of the Nile and in the water.

But Horus was prepared for them. Among his followers were many skilled smiths and metal-workers, and Horus had instructed them how to make weapons of iron tempered with many a spell. As the crocodiles and hippopotami drew near with open mouths, the smiths cast chains into the water so that

the fierce beasts entangled their legs and could be dragged towards the boats that followed the boat of Harmachis. And when they were near enough the smiths slew them with their spears, the iron points of which could pierce the thickest hide.

Then Horus and Harmachis changed themselves into great hawks which swooped down, one on the left bank of the river, and one on the right, and tore in pieces with their mighty talons all the followers of Set, whether they were in human form or in the guise of hippopotamus or crocodile.

So that war raged up and down the Nile, and many battles were fought in which Horus and his allies were victorious. At last Set himself came out against the boat of Harmachis, Set wearing the form of a monster with a hideous, animal head – a head that seemed to have been half-decayed, so that the accounts of the battle called Set 'The Stinking Head'.

The fight was long and terrible, but in the end Harmachis flung Set to the ground, smashing his face with his iron mace, bound him in chains, and brought him before the gods in council.

Then Ra said, 'Hand him over for punishment to Horus the son of Isis, and let them do unto him even as he did to Osiris.'

All the gods cried 'Yes!' to this. Thereupon Horus drew his sword and smote off the Stinking Head. Then he dragged the body of Set up and down Egypt, and at last cut him into fourteen pieces even as Set had torn the body of Osiris.

Yet the Evil One was not to be slain so easily. Before the sword of Horus fell, his wicked spirit had escaped from his body, imprisoning in it that of one of his chosen followers. And the spirit of Set entered into a poisonous black snake which crept away into a hole in the river bank.

Meanwhile Harmachis took upon himself the form of a mighty lion with a man's head, the head of a great Pharaoh of Egypt. His likeness is cut in stone at Giza, and the Greeks, when they came to Egypt thousands of years later, called it the

Sphinx. In this shape he raged up and down the land seeking out the followers of Set and slaying them with his mighty claws, no matter what disguise they took upon themselves.

For a little while it seemed that the war was over. But wise Thoth, looking through the distance as only he could, spoke to Horus saying: 'Son of Isis, the last battle is yet to be fought, even in this life. For Set is not dead. His spirit escaped ere ever you smashed the Stinking Head, and entered into a serpent. Now that cursed reptile has crept away into the desert far to the south, and Set is gathering allies and marching up the river to attack Egypt once more. Yet be of good heart, for the last battle shall be fought at Edfu, and there a temple shall be raised in honour of your victory that time shall not destroy.'

Then Horus gathered his forces once more and sailed up the Nile past Thebes, past Edfu itself, until he came to the island of Elephantinē. And there on the island stood Set himself in the form of a gigantic red hippopotamus. Opening his mouth he uttered a terrible curse:

'Let there come a raging tempest and a mighty flood against my enemies!' he cried, and his voice rolled in thunder down the valley of the Nile.

Then darkness fell upon the land, and a huge wave came roaring down from the First Cataract. It caught the fleet of Horus and swept it back down the river. Yet the boat in which Horus stood shone brightly through the darkness, and came to rest at Edfu not many miles below Elephantinē.

Set had been following, and now he paused, a vast red hippopotamus straddling the whole stream of the Nile. Against him Horus came sailing in his golden boat, wearing the likeness of a handsome youth twelve feet in height and holding ready a harpoon thirty feet long.

Set opened his mighty jaws to destroy Horus and his boat. But Horus cast his harpoon with such strong and deadly aim that it crashed through the roof of Set's mouth and deep into the brain beyond. And that one blow slew Set the Wicked One, the enemy of gods and men – and the red hippopotamus sank dead into the Nile at Edfu.

With the death of Set the darkness passed from the earth, and the people of Edfu came out to welcome Horus the Avenger and lead him to his shrine where the great temple now stands. And they sang the song of praise which the priests were to chant in after years when the great Festival of Horus was held annually at Edfu.

'Rejoice, dwellers in Edfu! The great god Horus, the lord of the heavens, has struck down the enemy of Osiris, he has avenged the death of his father! Eat the flesh of the vanquished, drink the blood of the red hippopotamus, burn his bones with fire! Let him be cut in pieces, and the scraps be given to the cats, and the offal cast to the reptiles!

'Glory to Horus of the mighty blow, the wielder of the harpoon, the brave one, the slayer of Set, the only son of Osiris, Horus of Edfu, Horus the Avenger!'

So there was peace in Egypt, and Horus reigned as Pharaoh for many hundreds of years, until the days when the great gods dwelt on earth were ended. Yet each Pharaoh who came after him, though but a man in body and in length of days, held the spirit of a god and was worshipped as such by his people. And the Egyptians embalmed the bodies of their dead kings and hid them away in mighty pyramids and deep tombs below the Valley of Kings at Western Thebes. For they knew that the day would come when Osiris and Horus would return to earth and fight the last and greatest battle against Set, and overcome him for ever. And that then all the dead who had lived virtuous lives and won through to the Duat, would return to earth with Osiris, and re-inhabit their bodies, and dwell forever in an Egypt purged of all wickedness – a fit home for the blessed.

Khnemu of the Nile

HORUS was the last of the great gods to reign as Pharaoh in Egypt, and when he had left the earth to ride across the sky with Ra in the Boat of the Sun, or visit his father Osiris in the Duat, the Land of the Dead, mortal men ruled in his place.

Every Pharaoh was, in spirit at least, the actual child of a god and was worshipped by his people as a god himself and credited with divine powers – even if sometimes he made mistakes like an ordinary mortal.

In the very early days of historical Egypt the Upper Kingdom and the Lower Kingdom were separate, and often at war with each other – and from this fact may have grown the myths of the battles between Set and Horus.

About the year 3200, however, the Pharaoh Menes united the Two Lands and combined the two sacred crowns into one, the 'Pschent' or Double Crown worn by all kings of Egypt down to the days of Cleopatra.

As every Pharaoh was thought of as a god, many stories grew up about their dealings with the gods, and one of the earliest concerned the great Zoser who lived about five hundred years after Menes had united the Two Lands.

It was Zoser who caused the first great pyramid to be built, the Step Pyramid at Saqqara on the edge of the desert above Memphis which stands to this day. His friend and adviser Imhotep, the world's first great architect, designed the pyramid for him and with it the great mile-long wall round the sanctuary at its foot, and in after days he too was worshipped as a god by the Egyptians.

Although Zoser had brought many blessings to the land, the god whom he had striven most to honour was himself, and instead of building temples and shrines to Ra or Thoth or

Osiris, he had thought only of making his own great sanctuary and pyramid.

In the tenth year of his reign the Nile did not rise as usual. The fields by the riverside in Upper Egypt, and the wide, flat plains of the Delta in Lower Egypt were not flooded and left covered with the rich mud in which wheat and barley grew so abundantly, and without which they would not grow at all.

At first this did not trouble the people greatly. The Nile was not always kind to them: sometimes there was a very small Inundation indeed, and occasionally the floods rose so high that houses and temples on either side were flooded. And, by the wisdom of Imhotep, Pharaoh had built barns and granaries and stored much grain in case such a bad year should come.

But when next year the Nile again did not rise when the time

of the Inundation was due, there were some murmurs, and bread was short that winter.

In all there were seven lean years in Egypt, and by the end of the seventh year starvation was everywhere in the land. No corn grew, the fruits dried up, the cattle grew thin and died of hunger. Every man robbed his neighbour when he could. The strong stole from the weak; old men and children were left to die; even the young grew so weak that they could scarcely put one foot before the other. The temples were shut up, for there was nothing to offer on the altars of the gods.

Then the people cried to Pharoah, the god on earth, to save them. They gathered outside his palace in Memphis, praying him to bring back the yearly Inundation and save them all from death.

Zoser was in despair for, god though he knew himself to be, he could not cause the Nile to rise, and all his prayers and incantations and sacrifices to the Nine Gods of Memphis were of no avail.

In despair he sent for Imhotep the wise: Imhotep, who, men said, must be the son of Ptah himself, Ptah the architect of the gods whose shrine was at Memphis, and said to him, 'Tell me what to do. Where is the secret birthplace of the Nile? Which god directs the flood? To what god must I turn?'

Then said Imhotep the wise: 'O Pharaoh – life, health, strength be to you! – I cannot answer this out of my own wisdom. But let me journey to Thebes to seek guidance from Thoth in whom is all knowledge. In the House of Life at Thebes are stored the sacred books called the Souls of Ra: it may be that Thoth the god of wisdom will guide me and show me an answer to your question written therein.'

So Imhotep journeyed with all haste up the Nile to Thebes. And Thoth granted his prayer, so that before long he was able to return in triumph to Zoser, before whom he fell down in worship, saying: 'O Pharaoh – life, health, strength be to you!

— Thoth has shown me all and instructed me in the hidden wisdom of our ancestors and the spells of the magicians who wrote in ancient days about the Inundation of the Nile.

'Harken to their wisdom, O Pharaoh! There lies in the Nile far to the south an island on which shall one day stand a great temple and a famous city. That island is called Elephantinē, and is the Beginning of the Beginning: for it was the first mound of dry land to rise out of the waters of Nun when Ra called the world into being, and on it he stood when he spoke the words of power and the First Name that made all things. There is a cave beneath the rock on which Elephantinē is raised above the waters of the Nile which flow on either side of it. It is called "The Fountain of Life"; it is also called "The Two Caverns" since it has two narrow mouths leading out beneath the surface of the Nile on either side. This is the mother that feeds all Egypt. This cave is the couch of the Nile; this is the birthplace of the River of Egypt. Here each year he retires and is reborn in strength. Hence he rushes out through the Two Caverns and floods all the land, so that his waters rise to forty feet in height at Elephantinē and to ten where they draw near the Great Green Sea. The god who dwells there is Khnemu: you have neglected him too long, and so have the people of Egypt.'

When Imhotep had finished speaking Zoser was glad, rejoicing that he had learned the secrets of Khnemu, god of the Nile. Yet he was still perplexed as to how he might win the favour of Khnemu and bring the Inundation once more to Egypt. So he spent the night in prayer and incantation in the great temple at Memphis, and in the darkness before the dawn Khnemu appeared to him, wearing the likeness of a tall man with a ram's head whose curling golden horns shone until the darkness of the shrine glowed as with molten fire.

'Know, you who for a little season dwell on earth as the Pharaoh of Egypt, that I am Khnemu the Fashioner!' cried the god. 'I guide the Nile and cause it to rise in the Fountain of Life and gush out through the Two Caverns beneath my sacred island of Elephantinē. When I lead the Nile over the fields of Egypt I give life to the corn – both barley and wheat grow rich and plentiful, there is spelt and emmer in abundance; the vines and the fruit trees flourish also – the grapes grow round and juicy to make the rich wines of Tanis and Mareotis; the figs and mulberries, dates and pomegranates grow large and sweet; the flowers bloom in the gardens and by the sacred pools of the gods – lotus and chrysanthemum, cornflower and mandrake. With my waters I bring life to men and women, by my power I fashion the shape of each even before their birth.

'But you have neglected the gods, and me you have not honoured at all: therefore the Nile has not risen and there have been seven lean years in Egypt. Bring back to the gods the honour and worship which is their due, and build for me such a temple as should rightly be mine, and the Nile will rise once more! It will pour forth for you year after year, nor ever cease to water and fertilize the fields of Egypt. Plants will grow, bent down by the weight of their fruits. Renenet, the goddess of harvest, the Lady of the Double Granary, will smile upon you as your fields grow golden with the ripening corn, and as you reap it and beat out the fat grains of wheat and barley on your threshing-floors. There shall be no more years of starvation and the granaries will never again be empty. Egypt will be a land of plenty and the hearts of your people shall be happier than ever before.'

When morning came Zoser ordered the Royal Barge to be made ready, bade Imhotep attend him, and set out in state up the Nile. Day and night his rowers bent to the oars, and oftimes the gentle breezes from the north filled the silken sails and helped him on his way.

Past Thebes he went and yet further to the south, beyond Edfu where Horus had slain Set, beyond Nubit (which we call

Kom Ombo) where stands the Temple of Harmachis and of Sobek the crocodile god, until he came to the island of Elephantinē that rises out of the Nile a little below Philae and the First Cataract.

And when he stood upon the high summit of sacred Elephantinē the Pharaoh Zoser uttered his decree.

'Let there be built here such a temple as was never before seen in Egypt. Let Imhotep the great architect lavish all his skill upon it, nor spare my treasuries to make it richer than any other temple. And when it is built, let it be the shrine and dwelling-place of Khnemu for ever. Moreover, the land on either side of the river, on the east and on the west, for many leagues, even from here to the neighbourhood of Nubit shall belong for ever to Khnemu, the good god who loves Egypt. And the wealth of the harvests gathered from his lands shall be offered to him and bring treasure to his temple so long as there is a Pharaoh in Egypt to guard the shrine of Khnemu on the sacred island of Elephantinē.'

Imhotep set to work to draw out the plans of the temple; and when mid-June of that year came the Nile began to rise and the waters to rush out of the Two Caverns until the whole land of Egypt was blessed with a great and fertile Inundation.

When the temple was built, Imhotep cut smooth the rock where it fell sheer into the river on the eastern side and marked it so that men might tell ever afterwards how high the Nile rose each year, and give thanks to Khnemu accordingly, or make greater sacrifices to him if the river were lower than usual. And this 'Nilometer' is there still, though the Temple of Khnemu is now but a heap of ruins.

But whenever Khnemu was neglected, the Inundation was small, and it was said that when men ceased to honour him and sought to cultivate the land of the Nile without his aid, a great misfortune would fall upon Egypt.

The Great Queen Hatshepsut

AMEN-RA, the King of the Gods, sat upon his throne and looked out upon Egypt. Presently he spoke to the assembled council of the gods – to Thoth and Khonsu and Khnemu, to Isis and Osiris, Nephthys, Horus, Harmachis, Anubis and the rest – saying: 'There has been many a Pharaoh in the Land of Khem, in the Double Land of Egypt, and some of them have been great and have pleased me well. Khufu and Khafra and Menkaura long ago who raised the great pyramids of Giza; Amen-hotep and Thutmose of today who have caused the peoples of the world to bow down at my feet. Now is the dawning of the golden age in Egypt, and it comes into my mind to create a great queen to rule over Khem: yes, I will unite the Two Lands in peace for her, I will give her rule over the whole world, over Syria and Nubia besides Egypt – yes, even to the far-distant land of Punt.'

Then said Isis in her silvery voice that sounded like the shaken bells on her sistrum, 'Father of Gods and Men, no queen has yet ruled in Egypt, in the holy land of Khem, save only I, when the good god Osiris had passed into the Duat, and the good god Horus was still but a child, while Set the Evil, the terrible one, stalked unchained up and down the land. Father of Gods and Men, if you create such a queen, my blessing and wisdom shall be upon her.'

Then Thoth spoke, Thoth the thrice-wise from whom no secrets were hid: 'O Amen-Ra, Lord of the Two Lands, King of the Gods, Maker of Men, harken to my words. In the royal palace at Thebes set in the Black Land, the rich country that Khnemu has made fertile with the dark mud of the Inundation, dwells a maiden. Ahmes is her name, and none in all the world is fairer than she nor more beautiful in all her limbs. She is the new-made bride of the good god Pharaoh Thutmose, who has but now returned to Thebes after his conquests beyond the Great Green Sea in the lands of the Syrians and the Apura. She alone can be the mother of the great queen whom you are about to create as ruler of the Two Lands. She rests alone in the palace of Pharaoh. Come, let us go to her.'

So Thoth took upon himself his favourite form, that of an ibis, in which he could fly swiftly through the air unrecognized by any. In this guise he flew into the palace of Thutmose at Thebes, to the great chamber with its painted walls where Queen Ahmes lay asleep.

Then Thoth cast a spell over the palace so that every living thing slumbered. Only the Pharaoh, King Thutmose himself, seemed to be awake – and yet it seemed that it was only his body which did not sleep. For, as if he were already dead, his three spiritual parts: the *Bai*, or soul; the *Ka*, or double, and the *Khou*, or spirit, left his body and gathered about it where it lay on the royal bed as they would in days to come when the good god Pharaoh Thutmose would be left to lie in his deep tomb chamber beneath the Valley of Kings until the coming of Osiris.

Yet the body of Thutmose now rose up from the bed, and the *Ka* took its place, lying there in the likeness of the King himself, while the *Bai*, like a bird with a human head, and the *Khou* in a tongue of flame, hovered over it.

Now for a space the body of Thutmose was the dwelling-place of Amen-Ra, the greatest of the gods, the maker and father of gods and men, and of all the earth. Great was his majesty and splendid his adornments. On his neck was the glittering collar of precious stones that only Pharaoh might wear, and on his arms were Pharaoh's bracelets of pure gold and electrum; but on his head were two plumes – and by these alone might it be known that here was Amen-Ra. Yet it seemed as if light shone from him, for as he passed through the dark palace, hall and chamber and corridor gleamed and faded in turn as if the sun shone in them for a space and then was veiled behind a cloud. And as he passed and faded there lingered behind him a scent as of the richest perfumes that come from the land of Punt.

He came to the sleeping-place of Queen Ahmes, and the double doors of ebony bound with silver opened before him and closed when he had passed. He found the Queen lying like a jewel on a golden couch that was shaped like a lion; he seated himself upon the couch, and he held to her nostrils Amen-Ra's divine symbol of life, and the breath of life passed into her as she breathed, and the couch rose and floated in the air. Then, waking or asleep, it seemed to Queen Ahmes that she was bathed in light so that she could see nothing above or below or round about her but the golden mist, save only the form of her husband the Pharaoh Thutmose who spoke in a voice that seemed to echo away into the distance, saying: 'Rejoice, most fortunate of women, for you shall bear a daughter who shall be the child of Amen-Ra, who shall reign over the Two Lands of Egypt and be sovereign of the whole world.'

Then Queen Ahmes sank into deep and dreamless sleep, while the form of Thutmose hastened back to where the *Bai* and the *Khou* hovered above the bed on which lay his *Ka*. A moment later Thutmose lay there sleeping as if nothing had happened, while the *Bai*, the *Ka* and the *Khou* had faded from mortal sight.

But Amen-Ra, Father of Gods and Men, summoned to him Khnemu the Fashioner and said, 'Mould clay upon your wheel, potter who forms the bodies of mankind, and make my daughter Hatshepsut who shall be born to Ahmes and Thutmose in the royal palace of Thebes.'

And when the time came Hatshepsut was born amid the rejoicing of all Egypt, and lay in her cradle beside the royal bed in the great room lit only by the moonlight.

Then once again the silence of deep sleep fell upon all the palace of Thebes. And presently the double doors opened of themselves and Amen-Ra entered in his own likeness attended by Hathor the goddess of love and her seven daughters, the Hathors, who weave the web of life for all who are born on this earth.

Then Amen-Ra blessed the baby Hatshepsut, taking her up in his arms and giving her the kiss of power so that she might indeed become a great queen, as his daughter should. And the Hathors wove the golden web of her life as Amen-Ra directed; and as they wove it seemed to pass before the eyes of Queen Ahmes so that she saw her daughter's life laid out before her.

She saw Hatshepsut as a beautiful girl kneeling in the temple at Karnak or Eastern Thebes while Amen-Ra and Horus poured the waters of purification upon her head, while the other gods and goddesses gathered in the shadows between the great columns to bless her. Then she saw Hatshepsut beside her human father Pharaoh Thutmose journeying through all the land of Egypt from Tanis on the Delta to Elephantinē in the south, hailed by all as the Great Queen to be. She saw Hatshepsut being crowned as Pharaoh of Egypt, the only woman ever to wear the Double Crown – save for Cleopatra the Greek who was to bring about Egypt's fall fifteen hundred years later. Then she saw her seated in state while the kings of the earth bowed down before her, bringing her gifts from the ends of the earth. And she saw Hatshepsut's great expedition to distant Punt – the ships sailing out of the Red Sea and far upon the waters of the ocean beyond to reach it on the coasts of central Africa: she saw the beehive huts of the black dwellers in Punt built on piles in the water and overshadowed by palms and incense trees with ladders leading up to the entrances. And then she saw the expedition returning to Egypt and bringing all the treasures from Punt to the Pharaoh Hatshepsut, and of how she dedicated them to her father Amen-Ra – Horus weighing the gold in his scales and Thoth writing down the measures of incense; and 'the good god' Hatshepsut herself offering the best of all she had before the ceremonial Boat of Amen-Ra that was carried by the priests of Thebes.

Last of all she saw the masons and the carvers and the artists fashioning the great mortuary temple of Hatshepsut, cutting out and painting on its walls all the pictures that she had seen in the Web of Fate the Hathors were weaving before her on this night of Hatshepsut's birth.

All things were fulfilled even as Queen Ahmes had seen, and Egypt reached its greatest glory under Hatshepsut and under her nephew Thutmose III who succeeded her. And all the tale is told in pictures and hieroglyphs in Der-el-Bahri, the mortuary temple of Hatshepsut in Western Thebes which still stands for all to see.

The Prince and the Sphinx

THERE was once a Prince in Egypt called Thutmose, who was a son of Pharaoh Amen-hotep, and the grandson of Thutmose III who succeeded the great Queen Hatshepsut. He had many brothers and half-brothers, and because he was Pharaoh's favourite son they were for ever plotting against him. Usually these plots were to make Pharaoh think that Thutmose was unworthy or unsuitable to succeed him; sometimes they were attempts to make the people or the priests believe that Thutmose was cruel or extravagant or did not honour the gods and so would make a bad ruler of Egypt; but once or twice the plots were aimed at his very life.

All this made Thutmose troubled and unhappy. He spent less and less of his time at Thebes or Memphis with Pharaoh's court, and more and more frequently rode on expeditions into Upper Egypt or across the desert to the seven great oases. And even when Pharaoh commanded his presence, or his position demanded that he must attend some great festival, he would slip away whenever he could with a few trusted followers, or even alone and in disguise, to hunt on the edge of the desert.

Thutmose was skilled in all manly exercises. He was a bowman who could plant arrow after arrow in the centre of the target; he was a skilled charioteer, and his horses were fleeter than the wind. Sometimes he would course antelopes for miles across the sandy stretches of desert; at others he would seek out the savage lions in their lairs among the rocks far up above the banks of the Nile.

One day, when the court was in residence at Memphis for the great festival of Ra at Heliopolis a few miles further down the Nile, Thutmose escaped from all the pomp and pageantry to hunt on the edge of the desert. He took with him only two servants, and he drove his own chariot up the steep road past Saqqara where the great Step Pyramid of Zoser stands, and away through the scrub and stunted trees where the cultivated land by the Nile faded into the stony waste and the stretches of sand and rock of the great Libyan desert.

They set off at the first glimmer of dawn so that they might have as much time as possible before the great heat of midday, and they coursed the gazelle northwards over the desert for many miles, parallel to the Nile but some miles away from it.

By the time the sun grew too hot for hunting Thutmose and his two followers had reached a point not very far away from the great Pyramids of Giza which the Pharaohs of the Fourth Dynasty had built over twelve hundred years before.

They stopped to rest under some palm trees. But presently Thutmose, desiring to be alone and wishing to make his prayer to the great god Harmachis, entered his chariot and drove away over the desert, bidding his servants wait for him.

Away sped Thutmose, for the sand was firm and smooth, and at last he drew near to the three pyramids of Khufu, Khafra and Menkaura towering up towards the sky, the burning sun of midday flashing on their golden peaks and glittering down their polished sides like ladders of light leading up to the Boat of Ra as it sailed across the sky.

Thutmose gazed in awe at these man-made mountains of stone. But most of all his attention was caught by a gigantic head and neck of stone that rose out of the sand between the greatest of the pyramids and a nearly-buried mortuary temple of huge squared stone blocks that stood on either side of the stone causeway leading from the distant Nile behind him right to the foot of the second pyramid – that of the Pharaoh Khafra.

This was a colossal carving of Harmachis the god of the rising sun, in the form of a lion with the head of a Pharaoh of Egypt – the form he had taken when he became the hunter of the followers of Set. Khafra had caused this 'sphinx' to be carved out of an outcrop of solid rock that happened to rise above the sand near the processional causeway leading from the Nile to his great pyramid. And he had bidden his sculptors shape the head and face of Harmachis in the likeness of his own.

During the long centuries since Khafra had been laid to rest in his pyramid the sands of the desert had blown against the Sphinx until it was almost buried. Thutmose could see no more than its head and shoulders, and a little ridge in the desert to mark the line of its back.

For a long while he stood looking up into the majestic face of the Sphinx, crowned with the royal crown of Egypt that had the cobra's head on its brow and which held in place the folds of embroidered linen which kept the sun from head and neck – only here the folds were of stone and only the head of the serpent fitted onto the carved rock was of gold.

The noonday sun beat mercilessly down upon Thutmose as he gazed up at the Sphinx and prayed to Harmachis for help in all his troubles.

Suddenly it seemed to him that the great stone image began to stir. It heaved and struggled as if trying in vain to throw off the sand which buried its body and paws, and the eyes were no longer carved stone inlaid with lapis lazuli, but shone with life and vision as they looked down upon him.

Then the Sphinx spoke to him in a great voice, and yet kindly as a father speaks to his son.

'Look upon me, Thutmose, Prince of Egypt, and know that I am Harmachis your father – the father of all Pharaohs of the Upper and Lower Lands. It rests with you to become Pharaoh indeed and wear upon your head the Double Crown of South and North; it rests with you whether or not you sit upon the throne of Egypt, and whether the peoples of the world come and kneel before you in homage. If you indeed become Pharaoh whatever is produced by the Two Lands shall be yours, together with the tribute from all the countries of the world. Besides all this, long years of life, health and strength shall be yours.

'Thutmose, my face is turned towards you, my heart inclines to you to bring you good things, your spirit shall be wrapped in mine. But see how the sand has closed in round me on every side: it smothers me, it holds me down, it hides me from your eyes. Promise me that you will do all that a good son should do for his father; prove to me that you are indeed my son and will help me. Draw near to me, and I will be with you always, I will guide you and make you great.'

Then, as Thutmose stepped forward the sun seemed to shine from the eyes of Harmachis the Sphinx so brightly that they dazzled him and the world went black and spun round him so that he fell insensible on the sand.

When he recovered the sun was sinking towards the summit of Khafra's pyramid and the shadow of the Sphinx lay over him.

Slowly he rose to his feet, and the vision he had seen came rushing back into his mind as he gazed at the great shape half-hidden in the sand which was already turning pink and purple in the evening light.

'Harmachis, my father!' he cried, 'I call upon you and all the gods of Egypt to bear witness to my oath. If I become Pharaoh, the first act of my reign shall be to free this your image from the sand and build a shrine to you and set in it a stone telling in the sacred writing of Khem of your command and how I fulfilled it.'

Then Thutmose turned to seek his chariot; and a moment later his servants, who had been anxiously searching for him, came riding up.

Thutmose rode back to Memphis, and from that day all went well with him. Very soon Amen-hotep the Pharaoh proclaimed him publicly as heir to the throne; and not very long afterwards Thutmose did indeed become King of Egypt – one of her greatest Kings, and the grandfather of her one great prophet and poet, Akhnaton.

Just a hundred and fifty years ago – 3,230 years after Thutmose IV became Pharaoh of Egypt – the Sphinx, again buried to the neck in sand, was dug out by an early archaeologist. Between its paws he found the remains of a shrine in which stood a red granite tablet fourteen feet high. Inscribed on it in hieroglyphs was the whole story of the Prince and the Sphinx. The tablet also tells us that it was set there in fulfilment of his vow by Pharaoh Thutmose IV in the third month of the first year of his reign, after he had cleared away all the sand which hid from sight Harmachis, the great Sphinx that had been made in the days of Khafra, when the world was young.

The Princess and the Demon

ABOUT a hundred years after Thutmose IV built his shrine to Harmachis between the paws of the Sphinx at Giza, Rameses the Great was Pharaoh of Egypt and overlord of all the lands from Libya in the west to Persia in the east, and from the land of the Hittites at the north of Syria to Babylon in the south.

Five years after he became Pharaoh he defeated the Hittites at the great Battle of Kadesh, and during the following sixty-two years of his reign he made journeys from time to time over his vast empire. When he did so he would dwell for a while in one city or another, and subject princes from the lands all about would bring him presents and tributes in token of their loyalty.

On a certain occasion, not many years after the Battle of Kadesh, Rameses was holding court in the great city of Babylon in the land of Mesopotamia, which the Egyptians called Nehern.

Kings and princes from far and wide, from one end of the Land of the Two Rivers to the other, came to do him homage. And they brought him gifts in tribute: gold and lapis lazuli, turquoise and rare woods. Each tried to outdo the other in the splendour and the rarity of their gifts.

But the Prince of Bekhten, besides his usual gifts of precious metals and scented woods, brought his eldest daughter and presented her to Rameses, saying, 'Life, health, strength be to you, Pharaoh of the world! Behold I bring as my tribute the most beautiful thing in all my kingdom, this princess my daughter.'

Rameses looked upon the girl and thought that she was indeed the most beautiful maiden in the world, fair in her limbs, tall and slender as a palm-tree. And as he looked, he loved her, and at once he spoke his decree: 'Prince of Bekhten, I accept your gift, the greatest and most precious that any of my subject kings has given me. And now behold, I give her a new name: Neferu-Ra, the Beauty of Ra, and I proclaim that she shall become my Great Royal Wife and be known as such throughout Egypt and all my domains. Scribes, write the name of Neferu-Ra in the cartouche, the royal oval, as that of a Great Queen, and let it be carved below mine in a place of honour in my new rock-hewn temple at Abu Simbel.'

All was done as he commanded, and when he returned to Egypt, Rameses continued to honour the Great Royal Wife, Queen Neferu-Ra, even as if she were the Queen of Egypt by right of birth.

Several years passed, and in the fifteenth of his reign

Rameses was in the mighty city of Thebes. It was the day of the great Festival of Amen-Ra when the boats go up and down the Nile with torches and lights, and the Sacred Barque of Ra, decorated with gold and precious stones, is carried from one temple to the next so that all people can see the image of Amen-Ra himself that is set therein.

Queen Neferu-Ra was with Pharaoh Rameses, and sat with him in the great temple, which today is called Karnak, to receive the gifts and worship of the people, and to hear any petitions that they wished to make.

Presently the Master of the King's Household came into the presence and bowing low cried, 'Life! Health! Strength! Pharaoh! Pharaoh! Pharaoh! An ambassador is here from the Prince of Bekhten, bringing rich presents for the Great Royal Wife, Neferu-Ra!'

'Let him come before my majesty and lay his gifts at our feet,' said Rameses.

When the ambassador entered he fell at the King's feet, kissing the ground in token of homage. And when he had presented the gifts from his royal master, he said, 'O Pharaoh, life, health, strength be to you! I bear a message from your servant the Prince of Bekhten. It concerns his daughter the Princess Bentresht, "Daughter of Joy", the little sister of the Great Royal Wife, Neferu-Ra. There has come a malady into her limbs, a strange sickness is upon her, nor may any in the Land of Nehern cure her, no, nor tell whence her sickness comes; and Babylon is famed for its wise men. Therefore my master prays you to send the wisest and most learned of the magicians of Egypt: for none in the world are more skilled in hidden things than the magicians of Khem.'

Pharaoh Rameses turned to his courtiers and said, 'Bring before me the most learned scribes of the House of Life, and the wisest of those who know of the hidden matters of the inner chambers of the temples of the gods.'

And when these had come before him, Rameses said, 'Listen to the message of the Prince of Bekhten, and when you have heard choose from among you the man most learned and skilful, to send into Nehern to cure Bentresht, the little sister of the Great Royal Wife, Neferu-Ra.'

When they had taken counsel among themselves, the wise men of Egypt chose Tehuti-em-heb, the Royal Scribe. And he set out straightway with the ambassador of the Prince of Bekhten; and after many months' journey he came to the land of Nehern and to the palace where Bentresht, the little sister of the Great Royal Wife, Neferu-Ra, lay sick.

Soon, by his magic, Tehuti-em-heb discovered that a demon had entered into the Princess Bentresht, and that all his power was of no avail against it – for the demon was hostile to him and would not be cast out.

Then said Tehuti-em-heb to the Prince of Bekhten, 'There is no man can cast out this demon. But my counsel is that you send once more to Egypt and beg the help of the great god Khonsu, the Expeller of Demons, whose temple is at Thebes.'

The Prince of Bekhten bade Tehuti-em-heb set out for Egypt at once as his messenger, and he sent with him a great and honourable guard, and many rich gifts to Khonsu.

When Rameses the Pharaoh heard the message which the Prince of Bekhten sent him, and when the Great Royal Wife, Neferu-Ra, had begged him to help her little sister, Bentresht, he went to the Temple of Khonsu in that part of Thebes which is now called Luxor.

In the innermost shrine of that wondrous temple, the shrine which none might enter save Pharaoh the good god and his chief priests, stood the great statue of Khonsu, the Moon-god, the Expeller of Demons. And in that shrine was also the little statue of Khonsu which the priests carried out to show to the people at the great Festival of Khonsu, when his image was borne in procession through the streets of Thebes and in the Holy Boat upon the Nile.

Rameses the King stood before the great statue of Khonsu, and prayed to the god, saying, 'Fair lord Khonsu, I come to you to beg you to save Bentresht, the little sister of the Great Royal Wife. Grant that the *Ka* of your spirit may enter into the image here and travel with it to Bekhten, there to drive out the demon which has entered into Bentresht and which will not depart from her even at the words of Tehuti-em-heb my great scribe and magician.'

Then the great statue of Khonsu inclined its head twice to show that Pharaoh's prayer was granted; and then it bowed twice more towards the lesser image – and the power of Khonsu, Expeller of Demons, passed into it.

Rameses came out of the Temple and told Tehuti-em-heb and the messengers of the Prince of Bekhten what had chanced.

And they set out rejoicing, carrying with them the little statue of Khonsu with all honour.

For many months they journeyed, and came at last to Bekhten. When he saw the image, the Prince of Bekhten fell on his knees before it and laid his forehead on the ground, crying, 'Glory be to Khonsu, Expeller of Demons, who has come to us! O, be kind to us according to the words and prayers of the good god Rameses, Pharaoh of Egypt!'

They brought Khonsu, the Expeller of Demons, into the bed-chamber of Bentresht, the little sister of the Great Royal Wife, Neferu-Ra. And at once the demon that was in her departed from her, and on the instant she was well and whole again.

The demon which had possessed the Princess Bentresht stood in the presence of Khonsu and said, 'You have come in peace, great god of Egypt, great Khonsu. Bekhten is now your city, its people bow down before you. I bow down before you, for I also am your slave. I will go now to that place from which I came, and trouble Bentresht, the little sister of the Great Royal Wife of Egypt no longer. But before I go, great Khonsu, I beg you to lay your commands upon the people of Bekhten that each year a holy day may be kept in my honour.'

'Let the Prince of Bekhten and his people make a great sacrifice for this demon,' cried Khonsu, 'and let them keep a day in his honour for ever more!'

The Prince and the people trembled and feared exceedingly when they heard Khonsu and the demon speaking; and they made haste to hold a holy day and offer sacrifices and hymns of praise.

The Princess Bentresht was well and happy again, and the demon troubled her no more. But the Prince of Bekhten wished to keep Khonsu, the Expeller of Demons, in his country to be his god and to bring many pilgrims. And he said to Tehuti-em-heb, 'Go with all the speed you may back to Egypt and tell Pharaoh Rameses – life, health, strength be to him! – that Bentresht, the little sister of the Great Royal Wife, Neferu-Ra, is freed from the demon by the power of Khonsu the Expeller of Demons. And when I have done honour to Khonsu, I will send his image with due attendance and rich gifts to make progress through all the lands so that the peoples of each may bow down to him and offer him worship on his way back to Thebes.'

Tehuti-em-heb returned with speed to Egypt. But the Prince of Bekhten did not send the image of Khonsu. He kept it in Bekhten for three years, four months and five days.

But at the end of that time, as he knelt in prayer before the image, Khonsu spoke suddenly, saying: 'My home is in Egypt, in the sacred city of Thebes – and thither will I go.'

And upon these words the *Ka* of the spirit of Khonsu flew out from the image in the form of a golden hawk, and sped like a beam of light over the mountains and the deserts towards Egypt.

The Prince of Bekhten was filled with fear, and dreaded the wrath of Khonsu and the other gods of Egypt.

So immediately he gave orders: 'The god Khonsu has left us. He has returned to Egypt. Therefore make haste and bear his dwelling back to Egypt also.'

Then the image was placed in a chariot loaded with gifts and all manner of beautiful things, and a great embassy set out with it towards Egypt. For many months they journeyed before they came at last to Thebes and entered the great Temple of Khonsu that stands in the Eastern Apt which we call Luxor.

Rameses the Pharaoh and Neferu-Ra, the Great Royal Wife, welcomed the little image of Khonsu. Together they set him once more in the sacred shrine of the temple, and all the rich gifts from Bekhten they set there also, dedicating them all to Khonsu and keeping none for themselves.

And the great god Khonsu, the Expeller of Demons, smiled upon Rameses the mighty Pharaoh, and upon Neferu-Ra, the Great Royal Wife, and upon Bentresht, the little sister in far-away Bekhten, and gave them health and prosperity all their days.

Tales of Magic

The Golden Lotus

SENEFERU, father of the Pharaoh Khufu who built the Great Pyramid of Giza, reigned long over a contented and peaceful Egypt. He had no foreign wars and few troubles at home, and with so little business of state he often found time hanging heavy on his hands.

One day he wandered wearily through his palace at Memphis, seeking for pleasures and finding none that would lighten his heart.

Then he bethought him of his Chief Magician, Zazamankh, and he said, 'If any man is able to entertain me and show me new marvels, surely it is the wise scribe of the rolls. Bring Zazamankh before me.'

Straightway his servants went to the House of Wisdom and brought Zazamankh to the presence of Pharaoh. And Seneferu said to him, 'I have sought throughout all my palace for some delight, and found none. Now of your wisdom devise something that will fill my heart with pleasure.'

Then said Zazamankh to him, 'O Pharaoh – life, health, strength be to you! – my counsel is that you go sailing upon the Nile, and upon the lake below Memphis. This will be no common voyage, if you will follow my advice in all things.'

'Believing that you will show me marvels, I will order out the Royal Boat,' said Seneferu. 'Yet I am weary of sailing upon the Nile and upon the lake.'

'This will be no common voyage,' Zazamankh assured him. 'For your rowers will be different from any you have seen at the oars before. They must be fair maidens from the Royal House of the King's Women: and as you watch them rowing, and see the birds upon the lake, the sweet fields and the green grass upon the banks, your heart will grow glad.'

'Indeed, this will be something new,' agreed Pharaoh, showing some interest at last. 'Therefore I give you charge of this expedition. Speak with my power, and command all that is necessary.'

Then said Zazamankh to the officers and attendants of Pharaoh Seneferu, 'Bring me twenty oars of ebony inlaid with gold, with blades of light wood inlaid with electrum. And choose for rowers the twenty fairest maidens in Pharaoh's household: twenty virgins slim and lovely, fair in their limbs, beautiful, and with flowing hair. And bring me twenty nets of golden thread, and give these nets to the fair maidens to be garments for them. And let them wear ornaments of gold and electrum and malachite.'

All was done according to the words of Zazamankh, and presently Pharaoh was seated in the Royal Boat while the maidens rowed him up and down the stream and upon the shining waters of the lake. And the heart of Seneferu was glad at the sight of the beautiful rowers at their unaccustomed task, and he seemed to be on a voyage in the golden days that were to be when Osiris returns to rule the earth.

But presently a mischance befell that gay and happy party upon the lake. In the raised stern of the Royal Boat two of the maidens were steering with great oars fastened to posts. Suddenly the handle of one of the oars brushed against the head of the girl who was using it and swept the golden lotus she wore on the fillet that held back her hair into the water, where it sank out of sight.

With a little cry she leant over and gazed after it. And as she ceased from her song, so did all the rowers on that side who were taking their time from her.

'Why have you ceased to row?' asked Pharaoh.

76

And they replied, 'Our little steerer has stopped, and leads us no longer.'

'And why have you ceased to steer and lead the rowers with your song?' asked Seneferu.

'Forgive me, Pharaoh – life, health, strength be to you!' she sobbed. 'But the oar struck my hair and brushed from it the beautiful golden lotus set with malachite which your majesty gave to me, and it has fallen into the water and is lost for ever.'

'Row on as before, and I will give you another,' said Seneferu.

But the girl continued to weep, saying, 'I want my golden lotus back, and no other!'

Then said Pharaoh, 'There is only one who can find the golden lotus that has sunk to the bottom of the lake. Bring to me Zazamankh my magician, he who thought of this voyage. Bring him here on to the Royal Boat before me.'

So Zazamankh was brought to where Seneferu sat in his silken pavilion on the Royal Boat. And as he knelt, Pharaoh said to him: 'Zazamankh, my friend and brother, I have done as you advised. My royal heart is refreshed and my eyes are delighted at the sight of these lovely rowers bending to their task. As we pass up and down on the waters of the lake, and they sing to me, while on the shore I see the trees and the flowers and the birds, I seem to be sailing into the golden days – either those of old when Ra ruled on earth, or those to come when the good god Osiris shall return from the Duat. But now a golden lotus has fallen from the hair of one of these maidens – fallen to the bottom of the lake. And she has ceased to sing and the rowers on her side cannot keep time with their oars. And she is not to be comforted with promises of other gifts, but weeps for her golden lotus. Zazamankh, I wish to give back the golden lotus to the little one here, and see the joy return to her eyes.'

'Pharaoh, my lord – life, health, strength be to you!'

answered Zazamankh the magician, 'I will do what you ask — for to one with my knowledge it is not a great thing. Yet maybe it is an enchantment you have never seen, and it will fill you with wonder, even as I promised, and make your heart rejoice yet further in new things.'

Then Zazamankh stood at the stern of the Royal Boat and began to chant great spells and words of power. And presently he held out his wand over the water, and the lake parted as if a piece had been cut out of it with a great sword. The lake here was twenty feet deep, and the piece of water that the magician moved rose up and set itself upon the surface of the lake so that there was a cliff of water on that side forty feet high.

Now the Royal Boat slid gently down into the great cleft in the lake until it rested on the bottom. On the side towards the forty-foot cliff of water there was a great open space where the bottom of the lake lay uncovered, as firm and dry as the land itself.

And there, just below the stern of the Royal Boat, lay the golden lotus.

With a cry of joy the maiden who had lost it sprang over the side on to the firm ground, picked it up and set it once more in her hair. Then she climbed swiftly back into the Royal Boat and took the steering oar into her hands once more.

Zazamankh slowly lowered his rod, and the Royal Boat slid up the side of the water until it was level with the surface once more. Then at another word of power, and as if drawn by the magician's rod, the great piece of water slid back into place, and the evening breeze rippled the still surface of the lake as if nothing out of the ordinary had happened.

But the heart of Pharaoh Seneferu rejoiced and was filled with wonder, and he cried: 'Zazamankh, my brother, you are the greatest and wisest of magicians! You have shown me wonders and delights this day, and your reward shall be all that you desire, and a place next to my own in Egypt.'

Then the Royal Boat sailed gently on over the lake in the glow of the evening, while the twenty lovely maidens in their garments of golden net, and the jewelled lotus flowers in their hair dipped their ebony and silver oars in the shimmering waters and sang sweetly a love song of old Egypt:

> 'She stands upon the further side,
> Between us flows the Nile;
> And in those waters deep and wide
> There lurks a crocodile.

'Yet is my love so true and sweet,
    A word of power, a charm –
The stream is land beneath my feet
    And bears me without harm.

'For I shall come to where she stands,
    No more be held apart;
And I shall take my darling's hands
    And draw her to my heart.'

Teta the Magician

THE Pharaoh Khufu reigned in Egypt and the building of the Great Pyramid at Giza had begun. His architect, Hemon, had learnt all the wisdom of Imhotep, who had built the Step Pyramid for Zoser a hundred years before, and the people of Egypt came in their thousands during the months of the Inundation each year when no farming was possible, and laboured gladly to the glory of the good god Pharaoh Khufu – who, like all true Pharaohs of Egypt, was held to be an incarnation of the spirit of Amen-Ra himself.

But there was one thing lacking. Hemon and the magicians of Memphis could not find the papyrus roll on which Imhotep was said to have written the words of power to keep a pyramid safe for ever against earthquake and thunderbolt – the weapons of Set the Evil One.

So Khufu sent out messengers and offered rewards to any who could find the words of power. The priests in the temples, from Philae to Tanis, searched their records; the magicians of Thebes and Abydos and Heliopolis sought the aid of spells and incantations – but all in vain.

At last, however, one of Pharaoh's sons, the Prince Hordedef, came to his father and bowing to the ground, said, 'Pharaoh my father – life, health, strength be to you! – I have found a magician stronger and more wonderful than any in your realm. His name is Teta and he dwells not far hence, at Meidum near the pyramid of your father Seneferu. There is no one like him in all Egypt: he is one hundred and ten years old, and was a boy when Zoser reigned and Imhotep built the first pyramid – and he eats five hundred bread-cakes and a side of beef, and drinks one hundred draughts of beer each day, even now. He knows how to restore the head that is smitten off; he knows how to make the savage lion of the desert follow him like a tame dog. And he swears that he knows how you may find the papyrus of Imhotep, inscribed with the words of power and the charms that must be spoken to keep a pyramid safe from the blows of Set the Evil One, who would destroy the dwelling places of the dead if they were not protected.'

Khufu the Pharaoh was delighted at this news, and said, 'Go in person, Hordedef my son, and take with you the Royal Litter and many attendants. Bring Teta the magician hither to Memphis with all speed, and treat him as if he were a subject prince visiting me his lord. Sail up the Nile in the Royal Boat so that Teta may travel with ease and comfort.'

So Hordedef set out in the Royal Boat, taking with him all things needful. Up the river he went, beyond Saqqara, beyond the Pyramids of Dahshur, until he came to the Pyramid of Meidum built by Seneferu. Here he landed and set out up the royal causeway to the Pyramid, and round it to the village beyond where dwelt Teta the magician.

They found the old man lying on a couch of palm-wood in the shade of his house, while his servants fanned him and anointed his head and feet with oil.

Prince Hordedef saluted him reverently, saying, 'Greetings worthy of your great and revered age be to you, Teta the magician, and may you continue free of the infirmities of the old. I come with a message from my father Khufu the great Pharaoh, life, health, strength be to him! He bids you visit him at Memphis and share the best of food and wine, even such as he himself eats and drinks. Moreover, he has sent his own Royal Boat so that you may travel in ease and comfort; and here is the Royal Litter of ebony set with gold in which you shall be carried, even as Pharaoh himself is borne, from here down to the Royal Boat, and from it to the palace in Memphis.'

Then Teta the magician replied, 'Peace be with you, Hordedef, son of the great Pharaoh, beloved of your father! May Khufu the Pharaoh – life, health, strength be to him! – advance you among his councillors and bring you all good things! May your *Ka* prevail against your enemies, and may your *Bai* find the road of righteousness that leads to the throne of Osiris in the Duat! I will come with you to the presence of Pharaoh. But let another boat follow bringing my attendants and the book of my art.'

All things were done as Teta desired, and in due time he sailed down the Nile in the Royal Boat and was carried in the Royal Litter to the palace at Memphis.

When Khufu heard of Teta's arrival he cried, 'Bring him before me immediately!' So Teta was led into the great Hall of Columns where Pharaoh awaited him on his throne with the great men of Egypt gathered about him.

Pharaoh said to Teta, 'How is it, great master of magic, that I have not seen you before?'

And Teta answered, 'He who is summoned is he who comes. The good god Pharaoh Khufu – life, health, strength be to him! – has sent for me, and behold I am here.'

Then Pharaoh said, 'Is it true, as I have heard tell, that you can restore to its place the head that is smitten off?'

And Teta replied, 'That indeed I can do, by the magic and wisdom of my hundred years and ten.'

'Bring from the prison one who is doomed to die,' commanded Khufu. 'And let the executioner come also to perform the death sentence on the criminal.'

But Teta exclaimed, 'Let it not be a man, O Pharaoh my lord. Let it be ordered that the head be smitten from some other living creature.'

So a duck was brought into the Hall of Columns and its head was cut off and laid at one end while its body remained at the other. Then Teta spoke the rolling words of power, and at his secret charm the duck's body fluttered along the ground, and its head moved likewise until they came together. And when the two parts met they joined, and the duck stood flapping its wings and quacking loudly.

Then a goose was brought, and the same magic was performed. And when an ox was beheaded Teta had but to speak the great words of power that made up his charm and the dead ox rose lowing to its feet and followed him across the Hall of Columns with its halter trailing on the ground.

Then said Pharaoh, 'All that is reported of you is true, Teta, greatest of magicians. But now can you tell me that which I long to know: where lies the papyrus on which Imhotep wrote the words of power that went to the building of the pyramid for Zoser, yes and for that of Seneferu my father also.'

'I can tell you where the papyrus lies,' answered Teta. 'It is in a casket of flint that is hidden in the great Temple of

Amen-Ra at Heliopolis. I cannot tell where that casket is concealed, but I know by my art that only one person can find the casket for you – yes, and I can tell you who it is.'

'Speak then, greatest of magicians!' exclaimed Khufu eagerly. 'And great indeed shall be your reward.'

'This very night,' answered Teta, 'the wife of a priest at Heliopolis shall bear three children at a birth, and the spirit of Amen-Ra shall be in them. Her name is Rud-didet, and one of her children shall find the casket . . . One of her children shall also sit where you sit and rule over Egypt.'

Then Khufu's heart was troubled, and he said, 'Surely it would be better to send and slay Rud-didet ere ever her children are born. For only by treachery can one of them become Pharaoh of Egypt.'

But Teta said, 'Let not your heart be troubled. Your son Khafra shall reign after you, and Menkaura his son after him, before a son of Rud-didet sits on the throne of the Upper and Lower Lands. The words of power can be found and spoken by none but he – and if he speaks them three great pyramids shall rise at Giza and stand there for ever. But if he speaks them not, all that you build, and your son builds and your son's son after him shall fall and crumble away and become as the sands of the desert.'

So Khufu issued a decree that the children of Rud-didet should dwell at Heliopolis in all honour, and that if any lifted a hand against them, be he a prince of Egypt, he should die a death of shame, and his body be destroyed so that his *Ka* should perish also. And he bade Hordedef take Teta the magician to dwell in his palace for the rest of his days, giving him daily five hundred bread-cakes, a hundred draughts of beer, a side of beef, and whatever else he might desire.

Meanwhile the three children of Rud-didet were born, and when the eldest, User-kaf, played in the temple of Amen-Ra as a boy he found the casket of flint in which was the papyrus roll containing the words of power. And, as a young priest, he read them at the dedication of the Great Pyramid of Khufu; as high priest of Heliopolis he read them at the dedication of the Pyramid of Khafra, and as Pharaoh-elect he read them at the dedication of the Pyramid of Menkaura. And when Menkaura was laid in his pyramid, User-kaf became Pharaoh of all Egypt – the first Pharaoh of the Fifth Dynasty.

As for the words of power and the charm against Set the Evil One, they seem to have done all that Khufu the Pharaoh wished: for the three great pyramids of Khufu, Khafra and Menkaura stand at Giza to this day – the first of the Seven Wonders of the ancient world, and the only one that is still standing nearly five thousand years later.

The Book of Thoth

RAMESES the Great, Pharaoh of Egypt, had a son called Setna who was learned in all the ancient writings, and a magician of note. While the other princes spent their days in hunting or in leading their father's armies to guard the distant parts of his empire, Setna was never so happy as when left alone to study.

Not only could he read even the most ancient hieroglyphic writings on the temple walls, but he was a scribe who could write quickly and easily all the many hundreds of signs that go to make up the ancient Egyptian language. Also he was a magician whom none could surpass: for he had learnt his art from the most secret of the ancient writings which even the priests of Amen-Ra, of Ptah and Thoth, could not read.

One day, as he pored over the ancient books written on the two sides of long rolls of papyrus, he came upon the story of another Pharaoh's son several hundred years earlier who had been as great a scribe and as wise a magician as he – greater and wiser, indeed, for Nefrekeptah had read the Book of Thoth by which a man might enchant both heaven and earth, and know the language of the birds and beasts.

When Setna read further that the Book of Thoth had been buried with Nefrekeptah in his royal tomb at Memphis, nothing would content him until he had found it and learnt all his wisdom.

So he sought out his brother Anherru and said to him, 'Help me to find the Book of Thoth. For without it life has no longer any meaning for me.'

'I will go with you and stand by your side through all dangers,' answered Anherru.

The two brothers set out for Memphis, and it was not hard

for them to find the tomb of Nefrekeptah the son of Amen-hotep, the first great Pharaoh of that name, who had reigned three hundred years before their day.

When Setna had made his way into the tomb, to the central chamber where Nefrekeptah was laid to rest, he found the body of the prince lying wrapped in its linen bands, still and awful in death. But beside it on the stone sarcophagus sat two ghostly figures, the *Kas*, or doubles, of a beautiful young woman and a boy – and between them, on the dead breast of Nefrekeptah lay the Book of Thoth.

Setna bowed reverently to the two *Kas*, and said, 'May Osiris have you in his keeping, dead son of a dead Pharaoh, Nefrekeptah the great scribe; and you also, who ever you be, whose *Kas* sit here beside him. Know that I am Setna, the priest of Ptah, son of Rameses the greatest Pharaoh of all – and I come for the Book of Thoth which was yours in your days on earth. I beg you to let me take it in peace – for if not, I have the power to take it by force or magic.'

Then said the *Ka* of the woman, 'Do not take the Book of Thoth, Setna, son of today's Pharaoh. It will bring you trouble even as it brought trouble upon Nefrekeptah who lies here, and upon me, Ahura his wife, whose body lies at Koptos on the edge of Eastern Thebes together with that of Merab our son – whose *Ka* you see before you, dwelling with the husband and father whom we loved so dearly. Listen to my tale, and beware!

'Nefrekeptah and I were the children of the Pharaoh Amen-hotep and, according to the custom, we became husband and wife, and this son Merab was born to us. Nefrekeptah cared above all things for the wisdom of the ancients and for the magic that is to be learned from all that is carved on the temple walls, and within the tombs and pyramids of long-dead kings and priests in Saqqara, the city of the dead that is all about us here on the edge of Memphis.

'One day as he was studying what is carved on the walls in one of the most ancient shrines of the gods, he heard a priest laugh mockingly and say, "All that you read there is but worthless. I could tell you where lies the Book of Thoth, which the god of wisdom wrote with his own hand. When you have read its first page you will be able to enchant the heaven and the earth, the abyss, the mountains and the sea; and you shall know what the birds and the beasts and the reptiles are saying. And when you have read the second page your eyes will behold all the secrets of the gods themselves, and read all that is hidden in the stars."

'Then said Nefrekeptah to the priest, "By the life of Pharaoh, tell me what you would have me do for you, and I will do it – if only you will tell me where the Book of Thoth is."

'And the priest answered, "If you would learn where it lies, you must first give me a hundred bars of silver for my funeral, and issue orders that when I die my body shall be buried like that of a great king."

'Nefrekeptah did all that the priest asked; and when he had received the bars of silver, he said, "The Book of Thoth lies beneath the middle of the Nile at Koptos, in an iron box. In the iron box is a box of bronze; in the bronze box is a sycamore box; in the sycamore box is an ivory and ebony box; in the ivory and ebony box is a silver box; in the silver box is a golden box – and in that lies the Book of Thoth. All around the iron box are twisted snakes and scorpions, and it is guarded by a serpent who cannot be slain."

'Nefrekeptah was beside himself with joy. He hastened home from the shrine and told me all that he had learned. But I feared lest evil should come of it, and said to him, "Do not go to Koptos to seek this book, for I know that it will bring great sorrow to you and to those you love." I tried in vain to hold Nefrekeptah back, but he shook me off and went to Pharaoh, our royal father, and told him what he had learnt from the priest.

'Then said Pharaoh, "What is it that you desire?" And Nefrekeptah answered, "Bid your servants make ready the Royal Boat, for I would sail south to Koptos with Ahura my wife and our son Merab to seek this book without delay."

'All was done as he wished, and we sailed up the Nile until we came to Koptos. And there the priests and priestesses of Isis came to welcome us and led us up to the Temple of Isis and Horus. Nefrekeptah made a great sacrifice of an ox, a goose and some wine, and we feasted with the priests and their wives in a fine house looking out upon the river.

'But on the morning of the fifth day, leaving me and Merab to watch from the window of the house, Nefrekeptah went down to the river and made a great enchantment.

'First he created a magic cabin that was full of men and tackle. He cast a spell on it, giving life and breath to the men, and he sank the magic cabin into the river. Then he filled the Royal Boat with sand and put out into the middle of the Nile until he came to the place below which the magic cabin lay. And he spoke words of power, and cried, "Workmen, workmen, work for me even where lies the Book of Thoth!" They toiled without ceasing by day and by night, and on the third day they reached the place where the Book lay. Then Nefrekeptah cast out the sand, and they raised the Book on it until it stood upon a shoal above the level of the river.

'And behold all about the iron box, below it and above it, snakes and scorpions twined. And the serpent that could not die was twined about the box itself. Nefrekeptah cried to the snakes and scorpions a loud and terrible cry – and at his words of magic they became still, nor could one of them move.

'Then Nefrekeptah walked unharmed among the snakes and scorpions until he came to where the serpent that could not die lay curled around the box of iron. The serpent reared itself up for battle, since no charm could work on it, and Nefrekeptah drew his sword and rushing upon it, smote off its head at a single blow. But at once the head and the body sprang together, and the serpent that could not die was whole again and ready for the fray. Once more Nefrekeptah smote off its head, and this time he cast it far away into the river. But at once the head returned to the body, and was joined to the neck, and the serpent that could not die was ready for its next battle.

'Nefrekeptah saw that the serpent could not be slain, but must be overcome by cunning. So once more he struck off its head. But before head and body could come together he put sand on each part so that when they tried to join they could not do so as there was sand between them – and the serpent that could not die lay helpless in two pieces.

'Then Nefrekeptah went to where the iron box lay on the shoal in the river; and the snakes and scorpions watched him; and the head of the serpent that could not die watched him also: but none of them could harm him.

'He opened the iron box and found in it a bronze box; he opened the bronze box and found in it a box of sycamore wood; he opened that and found a box of ivory and ebony, and in that a box of silver, and at the last a box of gold. And when he had opened the golden box he found in it the Book of Thoth. He opened the Book and read the first page – and at once he had power over the heavens and the earth, the abyss, the mountains and the sea; he knew what the birds and the beasts and the fishes were saying. He read the next page of spells, and saw the sun shining in the sky, the moon and the stars, and knew their secrets – and he saw also the gods themselves who are hidden from mortal sight.

'Then, rejoicing that the priest's words had proved true, and the Book of Thoth was his, he cast a spell upon the magic men, saying, "Workmen, workmen, work for me and take me back to the place from which I came!" They brought him back to Koptos where I sat waiting for him, taking neither food nor drink in my anxiety, but sitting stark and still like one who is gone to the grave.

'When Nefrekeptah came to me, he held out the Book of Thoth and I took it in my hands. And when I read the first page I also had power over the heavens and the earth, the abyss, the mountains and the sea; and I also knew what the birds, the beasts and the fishes were saying. And when I read the second page I saw the sun, the moon and the stars with all the gods, and knew their secrets even as he did.

'Then Nefrekeptah took a clean piece of papyrus and wrote on it all the spells from the Book of Thoth. He took a cup of beer and washed off the words into it and drank it so that the knowledge of the spells entered into his being. But I, who cannot write, do not remember all that is written in the Book of Thoth – for the spells which I had read in it were many and hard.

'After this we entered the Royal Boat and set sail for Memphis. But scarcely had we begun to move, when a sudden power seemed to seize our little boy Merab so that he was drawn into the river and sank out of sight. Seizing the Book of Thoth, Nefrekeptah read from it the necessary spell, and at once the body of Merab rose to the surface of the river and we lifted it on board. But not all the magic in the Book, nor that of any magician in Egypt, could bring Merab back to life. Nonetheless Nefrekeptah was able to make his *Ka* speak to us and tell us what had caused his death. And the *Ka* of Merab said, "Thoth the great god found that his Book had been taken, and he hastened before Amen-Ra, saying, 'Nefrekeptah, son of Pharaoh Amen-hotep, has found my magic box and slain its guards and taken my Book with all the magic that is in it.' And Ra replied to him, 'Deal with Nefrekeptah and all that is his as it seems good to you: I send out my power to work sorrow and bring a punishment upon him and upon his wife

and child.' And that power from Ra, passing through the will
of Thoth, drew me into the river and drowned me."

'Then we made great lamentation, for our hearts were well
nigh broken at the death of Merab. We put back to shore at
Koptos, and there his body was embalmed and laid in a tomb
as befitted him.

'When the rites of burial and the lamentations for the
dead were ended, Nefrekeptah said to me, "Let us now sail
with all haste down to Memphis to tell our father the Pharaoh
what has chanced. For his heart will be heavy at the death
of Merab. Yet he will rejoice that I have the Book of
Thoth."

'So we set sail once more in the Royal Boat. But when it
came to the place where Merab had fallen into the water, the
power of Ra came upon me also and I walked out of the cabin
and fell into the river and was drowned. And when Nefrekeptah by his magic arts had raised my body out of the river, and
my *Ka* had told him all, he turned back to Koptos and had my
body embalmed and laid in the tomb beside Merab.

'Then he set out once more in bitter sororw for Memphis.
But when it reached that city, and Pharaoh came aboard the
Royal Boat, it was to find Nefrekeptah lying dead in the cabin
with the Book of Thoth bound upon his breast. So there was
mourning throughout all the land of Egypt, and Nefrekeptah
was buried with all the rites and honours due to the son of
Pharaoh in this tomb where he now lies, and where my *Ka* and
the *Ka* of Merab come to watch over him.

'And now I have told you all the woe that has befallen us
because we took and read the Book of Thoth – the book which
you ask us to give up. It is not yours, you have no claim to it,
indeed for the sake of it we gave up our lives on earth.'

When Setna had listened to all the tale told by the *Ka* of
Ahura, he was filled with awe. But nevertheless the desire to
have the Book of Thoth was so strong upon him that he said,

'Give me that which lies upon the dead breast of Nefrekeptah, or I will take it by force.'

Then the *Kas* of Ahura and Merab drew away as if in fear of Setna the great magician. But the *Ka* of Nefrekeptah arose from out of his body and stepped towards him, saying, 'Setna, if after hearing all the tale which Ahura my wife has told you, yet you will take no warning, then the Book of Thoth must be yours. But first you must win it from me, if your skill is great enough, by playing a game of draughts with me – a game of fifty-two points. Dare you do this?'

And Setna answered, 'I am ready to play.'

So the board was set between them, and the game began. And Nefrekeptah won the first game from Setna, and put his spell upon him so that he sank into the ground to above the ankles. And when he won the second game, Setna sank to his waist in the ground. Once more they played and when Nefrekeptah won, Setna sank in the ground until only his head was visible. But he cried out to his brother who stood outside the tomb: 'Anherru! Make haste! Run to Pharaoh and beg of him the great Amulet of Ptah, for by it only can I be saved, if you set it upon my head before the last game is played and lost.'

So Anherru sped down the steep road from Saqqara to where Pharaoh sat in his palace at Memphis. And when he heard all, he hastened into the Temple of Ptah, took the great Amulet from its place in the sanctuary, and gave it to Anherru, saying: 'Go with all speed, my son, and rescue your brother Setna from this evil contest with the dead.'

Back to the tomb sped Anherru, and down through the passages to the tomb-chamber where the *Ka* of Nefrekeptah still played at draughts with Setna. And as he entered, Setna made his last move, and Nefrekeptah reached out his hand with a cry of triumph to make the final move that should win the game and sink Setna out of sight beneath the ground for

ever. But before Nefrekeptah could move the piece, Anherru leapt forward and placed the Amulet of Ptah on Setna's head. And at its touch Setna sprang out of the ground, snatched the Book of Thoth from Nefrekeptah's body and fled with Anherru from the tomb.

As they went they heard the *Ka* of Ahura cry, 'Alas, all power is gone from him who lies in this tomb.'

But the *Ka* of Nefrekeptah answered, 'Be not sad: I will make Setna bring back the Book of Thoth, and come as a suppliant to my tomb with a forked stick in his hand and a fire-pan on his head.'

Then Setna and Anherru were outside, and at once the tomb closed behind them and seemed as if it had never been opened.

When Setna stood before his father the great Pharaoh and told him all that had happened, and gave him the Amulet of Ptah, Rameses said, 'My son, I counsel you to take back the Book of Thoth to the tomb of Nefrekeptah like a wise and

95

prudent man. For otherwise be sure that he will bring sorrow and evil upon you, and at the last you will be forced to carry it back as a suppliant with a forked stick in your hand and a fire-pan on your head.'

But Setna would not listen to such advice. Instead, he returned to his own dwelling and spent all his time reading the Book of Thoth and studying all the spells contained in it. And often he would carry it into the Temple of Ptah and read from it to those who sought his wisdom.

One day as he sat in a shady colonnade of the temple he saw a maiden, more beautiful than any he had ever seen, entering the temple with fifty-two girls in attendance on her. Setna gazed fascinated at this lovely creature with her golden girdle and head-dress of gold and coloured jewels, who knelt to make her offerings before the statue of Ptah. Soon he learnt that she was called Tabubua, and was the daughter of the high priest of the cat-goddess Bastet from the city of Bubastis to the north of Memphis – Bastet who was the bride of the god Ptah of Memphis.

As soon as Setna beheld Tabubua it seemed as if Hathor the goddess of love had cast a spell over him. He forgot all else, even the Book of Thoth, and desired only to win her. And it did not seem as if his suit would be in vain, for when he sent a message to her, she replied that if he wished to seek her he was free to do so – provided he came secretly to her palace in the desert outside Bubastis.

Setna made his way thither in haste, and found a pylon tower in a great garden with a high wall round about it. There Tabubua welcomed him with sweet words and looks, led him to her chamber in the pylon and served him with wine in a golden cup.

When he spoke to her of his love, she answered, 'Be joyful, my sweet lord, for I am destined to be your bride. But remember that I am no common woman but the child of Bastet the

Beautiful – and I cannot endure a rival. So before we are wed write me a scroll of divorcement against your present wife; and write also that you give your children to me to be slain and thrown down to the cats of Bastet – for I cannot endure that they shall live and perhaps plot evil against our children.'

'Be it as you wish!' cried Setna. And straightway he took his brush and wrote that Tabubua might cast his wife out to starve and slay his children to feed the sacred cats of Bastet. And when he had done this, she handed him the cup once more and stood before him in all her loveliness, singing a bridal hymn. Presently terrible cries came floating up to the high window of the pylon – the dying cries of his children, for he recognized each voice as it called to him in agony and then was still.

But Setna drained the golden cup and turned to Tabubua, saying, 'My wife is a beggar and my children lie dead at the pylon foot, I have nothing left in the world but you – and I would give all again for you. Come to me, my love!'

Then Tabubua came towards him with outstretched arms, more lovely and desirable than Hathor herself. With a cry of ecstasy Setna caught her to him – and as he did so, on a sudden she changed and faded until his arms held a hideous, withered corpse. Setna cried aloud in terror, and as he did so the darkness swirled around him, the pylon seemed to crumble away, and when he regained his senses he found himself lying naked in the desert beside the road that led from Bubastis to Memphis.

The passers-by on the road mocked at Setna. But one kinder than the rest threw him an old cloak, and with this about him he came back to Memphis like a beggar.

When he reached his own dwelling place and found his wife and children there alive and well, he had but one thought and that was to return the Book of Thoth to Nefrekeptah.

'If Tabubua and all her sorceries were but a dream,' he

exclaimed, 'they show me in what terrible danger I stand. For if such another spell is cast upon me, next time it will prove to be no dream.'

So, with the Book of Thoth in his hands, he went before Pharaoh his father and told him what had happened. And Rameses the Great said to him, 'Setna, what I warned you of has come to pass. You would have done better to obey my wishes sooner. Nefrekeptah will certainly kill you if you do not take back the Book of Thoth to where you found it. Therefore go to the tomb as a suppliant, carrying a forked stick in your hand and a fire-pan on your head.'

Setna did as Pharaoh advised. When he came to the tomb and spoke the spell, it opened to him as before, and he went down to the tomb-chamber and found Nefrekeptah lying in his sarcophagus with the *Kas* of Ahura and Merab sitting on either side. And the *Ka* of Ahura said, 'Truly it is Ptah, the great god, who has saved you and made it possible for you to return here as a suppliant.'

Then the *Ka* of Nefrekeptah rose from the body and laughed, saying, 'I told you that you would return as a suppliant, bringing the Book of Thoth. Place it now upon my body where it lay these many years. But do not think that you are yet free of my vengeance. Unless you perform that which I bid you, the dream of Tabubua will be turned into reality.'

Then said Setna, bowing low, 'Nefrekeptah, master of magic, tell me what I may do to turn away your just vengeance. If it be such as a man may perform, I will do it for you.'

'I ask only a little thing,' answered the *Ka* of Nefrekeptah. 'You know that while my body lies here for you to see, the bodies of Ahura and Merab rest in their tomb at Koptos. Bring their bodies here to rest with mine until the Day of Awakening when Osiris returns to earth – for we love one another and would not be parted.'

Then Setna went in haste to Pharaoh and begged for the use

of the Royal Boat. And Pharaoh was pleased to give command that it should sail with Setna where he would. So Setna voyaged up the Nile to Koptos. And there he made a great sacrifice to Isis and Horus, and begged the priests of the temple to tell him where Ahura and Merab lay buried. But, though they searched the ancient writings in the temple, they could find no record.

Setna was in despair. But he offered a great reward to any who could help him, and presently a very old man came tottering up to the temple and said, 'If you are Setna the great scribe, come with me. For when I was a little child my grandfather's father who was as old as I am now told me that when he was even as I was then his grandfather's father had shown him where Ahura and Merab lay buried – for as a young man in the days of Pharaoh Amen-hotep the First he had helped to lay them in the tomb.'

Setna followed eagerly where the old man led him, and came to a house on the edge of Koptos.

'You must pull down this house and dig beneath it,' said the old man. And when Setna had bought the house for a great sum from the scribe who lived in it, he bade the soldiers whom Pharaoh had sent with him level the house with the ground and dig beneath where it had stood.

They did as he bade them, and presently came to a tomb buried beneath the sand and cut from the rock. And in it lay the bodies of Ahura and Merab. When he saw them, the old man raised his arms and cried aloud; and as he cried he faded from sight and Setna knew that it was the *Ka* of Nefre-keptah which had taken on that shape to lead him to the tomb.

So he took up the mummies of Ahura and Merab and conveyed them with all honour, as if they had been the bodies of a queen and prince of Egypt, down the Nile in the Royal Boat to Memphis.

And there Pharaoh himself led the funeral procession to

Saqqara, and Setna placed the bodies of Ahura and Merab beside that of Nefrekeptah in the secret tomb where lay the Book of Thoth.

When the funeral procession had left the tomb, Setna spoke a charm and the wall closed behind him leaving no trace of a door. Then at Pharaoh's command they heaped sand over the low stone shrine where the entrance to the tomb was hidden; and before long a sandstorm turned it into a great mound, and then levelled it out so that never again could anyone find a trace of the tomb where Nefrekeptah lay with Ahura and Merab and the Book of Thoth, waiting for the Day of Awakening when Osiris shall return to rule over the earth.

Se-Osiris and the Sealed Letter

MANY tales were told in Ancient Egypt of Setna, the son of Rameses the Great, who was the wisest of all scribes, and who found and read the Book of Thoth. And tales were told also of his son Se-Osiris – 'the Gift of Osiris' – the wonderful child who, at the age of twelve, was the greatest magician Egypt had ever known.

His most famous exploit began on a day when Rameses sat in the great hall of his palace at Thebes with his princes and nobles about him, and the Grand Vizier came bustling in with a look of shocked surprise on his face and prostrated himself before Rameses, crying: 'Life, health, strength be with you, O Pharaoh! There has come to your court a rascally Ethiopian seven feet tall who demands speech with you, saying that he is here to prove that the magic of Egypt is nothing compared with the magic of Ethiopia.'

'Bid him enter,' commanded Pharaoh, and presently a huge Ethiopian strode into his presence, bowed to the ground, and said: 'King of Egypt, I have brought here in my hand a sealed letter to see if any of your priests or scribes or magicians can read what is written in it without breaking the seal. And if none of them can read it, I will go back to Ethiopia and tell my king and all his people how weak is the magic of the Egyptians, and you will be a jest on the lips of all men.'

Pharaoh was both angry and troubled when he heard this, and he sent in haste for his wise son Setna and told him what had chanced. Setna also was dismayed, but he said, 'O Pharaoh, my father – life, health, strength be to you! – bid this barbarian go and take his rest; let him eat, drink and sleep in the Royal Guest-House until your court is assembled next, when I will bring a magician who will show that we who practise the magic art in Egypt are a match for anyone from the lands beyond Kush.'

'Be it so,' answered Pharaoh, and the Ethiopian was led away to the hospitable entertainment of the Royal Guest-House.

But although he had spoken so confidently, Setna was troubled. Though he had read the Book of Thoth and was the wisest man in Egypt and the most skilled magician, he could not read a letter that was written on a papyrus scroll that was rolled up and sealed without breaking the seal and unrolling the letter.

When he returned to his palace he lay down on his couch to think; and he looked so pale and troubled that his wife came to him fearing that he was ill. With her came their son Se-Osiris, and when Setna had told all his trouble the woman burst into tears but the boy began to laugh gleefully.

'My son,' said Setna with a puzzled look, 'why do you laugh when I tell you of that which has caused so much concern to Pharaoh and such sorrow to me your father?'

'I laugh,' answered Se-Osiris, 'because your trouble is no trouble at all but a gift of the gods to bring great glory to Egypt and humble the proud overbearing King of Ethiopia and his wizards. Cease from sorrow. I will read the sealed letter.'

Setna sprang up and looked searchingly at the small boy who stood so confidently before him.

'You have great powers of magic, I know, my son,' he said. 'But how can I be certain that when we stand before Pharaoh you can indeed read that which is written on a sealed roll of papyrus?'

'Go to your room where your writings are kept,' answered Se-Osiris. 'Choose any papyrus that you like, seal it if it is not sealed already, and I will read it to you without even taking it out of your hand.'

Setna sprang up and fetched a papyrus from his study. And

Se-Osiris read what was written on it while his father held it still rolled and sealed with wax.

Next day Pharaoh Rameses summoned his court once more. When all were assembled he bade the Grand Vizier bring the Ethiopian before him with his sealed letter.

Proudly the huge wizard strode into the hall and with hardly a nod to the greatest of all the Pharaohs, he held up the roll of papyrus and cried: 'King of Egypt, let your magicians read what is written in this sealed letter – or else admit that the magic of Ethiopia is greater than the magic of Egypt!'

'Setna, my son,' said Pharaoh, 'you are the greatest magician in Egypt: be pleased to answer this insolent barbarian who, if he were not a messenger, I would have beaten with rods.'

'O Pharaoh – life, health, strength be to you!' answered Setna. 'Such a dog as this, who has no reverence for the good god Pharaoh Rameses Usi-ma-res, is not worthy to be pitted against a magician full of years and wisdom. But my son Se-Osiris who, at the age of twelve, is already skilled enough in the secret lore to stand against him, shall read his letter.'

There was a murmur throughout the court and a little ripple of laughter as the small boy stepped forward on one side of Pharaoh's throne and came down to the gigantic Ethiopian who stood scowling at the foot of the dais with the sealed letter held up in his right hand.

'O Pharaoh my grandfather – life, health, strength be to you!' said Se-Osiris in a clear voice that all could hear. 'The sealed roll in this wizard's hand tells the tale of an insult wrought upon one who held the scourge and the crook, one who wore the Double Crown – a Pharaoh of Egypt who sat where you sit five hundred years ago.

'It tells of a king who ruled as today's king rules over the Ethiopians. He sat one day in his marble summer-house beside the river Nile far away to the south. Between the pillars behind him was a trellis of ebony, and it was grown so thickly with sweet-smelling creepers that it seemed like a thick hedge. In the shade behind it his greatest magicians sat talking together, and the King, listening idly to their words, heard the first say, "In arms we may not be able to stand against Egypt, but in magic we are certainly the masters of Pharaoh our overlord and all his people. Why, even I could bring a great darkness over all the land of Egypt that would last for three days."

' "True," said another magician. "I, for example, could bring a blight upon Egypt that would destroy its crops for one season."

'So they went on, each telling of the plague that he could bring upon Egypt, until at last the chief magicians of Ethiopia said, "As for this dog of a Pharaoh who calls himself our overlord, I could bring him here by magic and cause him to be

beaten with five hundred strokes of the rod before all the people. Yes, I could do this and carry him back to his palace in Egypt all in the space of five hours."

'When the King heard this, he summoned the magicians before him, and said to the chief of them, "Son of Tnahsit, I have heard your words. If you do to the Pharaoh of Egypt even as you have said, I will give you a greater reward than any magician has ever received."

'The Son of Tnahsit bowed before him and at once set about his spells. He fashioned a litter and four bearers in wax; he chanted words of power over them and he breathed the breath of life into them, and he bade them hasten to Egypt and bring Pharaoh to Ethiopia during the dark hours of that night.'

When he had read so far in the sealed letter, Se-Osiris turned to the Ethiopian and said, 'These words that I have read, are they not written in the sealed roll that you hold in your hands? Answer truly, or may Amen-Ra blast you where you stand!'

The Ethiopian bowed before Se-Osiris and gasped, 'These words are indeed written there, my lord.'

So Se-Osiris continued reading from the sealed letter: 'All happened as the Son of Tnahsit had promised. Pharaoh was lifted from his royal bed at Thebes, carried to Ethiopia, beaten in public by the King's servants with five hundred strokes, and taken back again all in the space of five hours. The next morning he woke in great pain, and the marks of the rods on his back told him that it had been no dream.

'So Pharaoh summoned his court and called his magicians before him and told them of the shame that had been wrought.

' "I desire vengeance upon the King of Ethiopia," he ended, "and vengeance upon his magicians. Moreover I wish the land of Egypt and the divine person of her Pharaoh to be protected against these barbarians and their evil and insulting magic."

'Then Pharaoh's Chief Magician, the Kherheb of Egypt, bowed low before him, crying, "O Pharaoh – life, health, strength be to you! – it cannot be that this wickedness of the sons of Set who dwell in Nubia and Ethiopia shall continue against your divine majesty. Tonight I shall seek counsel of Thoth, the god of wisdom and magic, in his great temple; and tomorrow be sure, I shall have a charm that will bring both vengeance and protection."

'So the Kherheb slept in the temple that night, and Thoth with the ibis-head came and stood over his bed and instructed him in all that was to be done for the honour of Egypt and the protection of the good god her Pharaoh.

'No Ethiopian litter-bearers had visited the royal palace that night; but the night after they came again to carry Pharaoh into Ethiopia to be beaten before all the barbarians. But the magic which Thoth the wise had taught to the Kherheb of Egypt was so strong that their magic was in vain. They could but stand and gibber in the royal bed-chamber: they could not so much as raise their arms to lift Pharaoh on to the magic litter. And presently they faded away and were no more seen in Egypt.

'But next morning, when the Kherheb heard of what had chanced in Pharaoh's bed-chamber he rejoiced exceedingly. And straightway he set about preparing a magic litter of his own, with four bearers who that night carried the King of Ethiopia into the great square before the Temple of Amen-Ra at Thebes and had him beaten with five hundred strokes of the rod before all the people there assembled.

'In the morning the King of Ethiopia woke in his palace sore and troubled. At once he sent for the Son of Tnahsit and bade him find a magic to protect him against the magicians of Egypt and bring vengeance upon Pharaoh.

'But the Son of Tnahsit could do nothing. Three times was the King of Ethiopia carried to Thebes and beaten before all the people. Then he humbled himself before the glory of the good god Pharaoh and was beaten no more. But he caused the Son of Tnahsit to be cast out of his palace with many curses, saying, "In life and in death may you wander the earth until you bring vengeance upon Egypt, upon her Pharaoh and upon her magicians – and until you prove that there is a magic greater than the magic of the magicians of Khem."'

Then Se-Osiris pointed to the sealed letter, saying, 'Ethiopian, these words which I have read, are they not written in the roll of papyrus which you hold, still sealed, in your hands? Answer truly, or may Amen-Ra blast you where you stand.'

The Ethiopian fell upon his knees and cried, 'These words are indeed written there, mighty magician!'

Then the seal was broken and the letter was read out loud before Pharaoh and all his court. And the words of the letter were the words Se-Osiris the wonderful child had read: only that, in reading, he had paid due honour to Pharaoh, and had spoken of the barbarians of Ethiopia in such terms as were proper.

After this the Ethiopian said humbly, 'Mighty Pharaoh, lord of Egypt and overlord of Ethiopia, may I go hence in peace?'

But Se-Osiris spoke quickly, saying, 'Oh Pharaoh – life, health, strength be to you! – this wizard who kneels before you has within him the *Bai* of the Son of Tnahsit. Yes, he is the wizard who wrought such shame upon him who sat upon the throne of the Two Lands and held the scourge and the crook five hundred years ago. Is it not right that the battle between the magic of Ethiopia and the magic of Egypt should be fought out to the finish here and now before your eyes?'

Pharaoh Rameses the Great nodded his head and touched his grandson the wonderful child Se-Osiris with his sceptre, saying, 'Kherheb of today, finish that which the Kherheb of five centuries ago began.' Then to the giant Ethiopian he cried,

'Black dog of the south, if you have magic to match against the magic of Egypt, show it now!'

The Ethiopian laughed grimly. 'White dog of the north!' he cried. 'I defy you! I have such magic at my command that presently Set will take you as his own, and Apophis the Devourer of Souls will soon be feasting up the *Bai* of that which was once a Pharaoh of Egypt. Behold!'

The Ethiopian waved the sealed roll as if it had been a wand, and pointed to the floor in front of Pharaoh, muttering a great word of power.

At once there reared up a mighty serpent hissing loudly, its forked tongue flickering evilly and its poisoned fangs bared to kill.

Pharaoh cowered back with a cry. But Se-Osiris laughed merrily, and as he raised his hand the giant cobra dwindled into a little white worm which he picked up between his thumb and first finger and cast out of the window.

The Ethiopian uttered a howl of rage and waved his arms, spitting curses mingled with incantations as he did. At once a cloud of darkness descended upon the great hall, as black as midnight in a tomb and as dense as the smoke of burning bodies.

But Se-Osiris laughed again. Then he took the darkness in his hands, crushed it together until it was no bigger than a ball such as children make of the dark clay beside the Nile, and tossed it out of the window.

A third time the Ethiopian waved his arms, and this time he yelled as if the jaws of Apophis had already closed upon him. At once a great sheet of fierce flame leapt up from the floor and moved forward as if to consume Pharaoh and all who stood beside him on the royal dais.

But Se-Osiris laughed for the third time. Then he blew upon the sheet of flame, and it drew back and wrapped itself about the Ethiopian. There was one great cry, and then the flame dwindled and went out like a candle when all the wax is burnt away.

On the floor in front of Pharaoh lay only a little pile of ash; and Se-Osiris said quietly, 'Farewell to the Son of Tnahsit! May his *Bai* dwell elsewhere for ever, and come not again to trouble Egypt or insult the good god Pharaoh – life, health, strength be to him!'

The Land of the Dead

THE one visit to the Duat of which a record remains was paid by Se-Osiris, the wonderful child magician who read the sealed letter, and his father Setna, the son of Pharaoh Rameses the Great.

They stood one day in the window of the palace at Thebes watching two funerals on their way to the West. The first was that of a rich man: his mummy was enclosed in a wooden case inlaid with gold; troops of servants and mourners carried him to burial and bore gifts for the tomb, while many priests walked in front and behind chanting hymns to the gods and reciting the great names and words of power which he would need on his journey through the Duat.

The second funeral was that of a poor labourer. His two sons carried the simple wooden case: his widow and daughters-in-law were the only mourners.

'Well,' said Setna, watching the two funerals going down to where the boats were waiting to carry them across the Nile, 'I hope that my fate will be that of the rich noble and not of the poor labourer.'

'On the contrary,' said Se-Osiris, 'I pray that the poor man's fate may be yours and not that of the rich man!'

Setna was much hurt by his son's words, but Se-Osiris tried to explain them, saying, 'Whatever you may have seen here matters little compared with what will chance to these two in the Judgement Hall of Osiris. I will prove it to you, if you will trust yourself to me. I know the words of power that open all gates: I can release your *Bai* and mine – our souls, that can then fly into the Duat, the world of the dead, and see all that is happening there. Then you will discover how different are the fates of this rich man who has worked evil during his life, and this poor man who has done nothing but good.'

Setna had learnt to believe anything the wonderful child said without surprise, and now he agreed to accompany his son into the Duat, even though he knew that such an expedition would be dangerous: for once there they might not be able to return.

So the prince and the small boy made their way into the sanctuary of the Temple of Osiris where, as members of the royal family, they had power to go.

When Setna had barred the doors, Se-Osiris drew a magic circle round them and round the statue of Osiris and round the altar on which a small fire of cedar wood was burning. Then he threw a certain powder into the flame upon the altar. Thrice he threw the powder, and as he threw it a ball of fire rose from the altar and floated away. Then he spoke a spell and ended with a great name of power, a word at which the whole temple rocked and the flame on the altar leapt high, and then sank into darkness.

But the Temple of Osiris was not dark. Setna turned to see whence the light came – and would have cried out in horror if the silence had not pressed upon him like a weight that held him paralysed.

For standing on either side of the altar he saw himself and his son Se-Osiris: only suddenly he knew that it was not his own body and the boy's – for the two bodies lay in the shadows cast by these two forms – the forms of their *Kas* or doubles, and above each *Ka* hovered a tongue of flame which was its *Khou* or spirit – and the clear light of the *Khou* served to show its *Ka* and the dim form of the body from which *Ka* and *Khou* were drawn.

Then the silence was broken by a whisper soft as a feather falling, yet which seemed to fill the whole Temple with sound: 'Follow me now, my father,' said the voice of Se-Osiris, 'for the time is short and we must be back before the morning if we would live to see the Sun of Ra rise again over Egypt.'

Setna turned, and saw beside him the *Bai* or soul of Se-Osiris – a great bird with golden feathers but with the head of his son.

'I follow,' he forced his lips to answer; then, as the whisper filled the Temple, he rose on the golden wings of his own *Bai* and followed the *Bai* of Se-Osiris.

The temple roof seemed to open to let them through, and a moment later they were speeding into the West swifter than an arrow from an Ethiop's bow.

Darkness lay over Egypt, but one red gash of sunset shone through the great pass in the mountains of the Western Desert, the Gap of Abydos. Through this they sped into the First Region of the Night and saw beneath them the Mesektet Boat in which Ra began his journey into the Duat with the ending of each day. Splendid was the Boat, glorious its trappings, and its colours were of amethyst and emerald, jasper and turquoise, lazuli and the deep glow of gold. A company of the gods drew the Boat along the ghostly River of Death with golden towing-ropes; the portals of the Duat were flung wide, and they entered the First Region between the six serpents who were curled on either side. And in the great Boat of Ra journeyed the *Kas* of all those who had died that day and were on their way to the Judgement Hall of Osiris.

So the Boat moved on its way through regions of night and thick darkness and came to the portal of the Second Region. Tall were the walls on either side, and upon their tops were the points of spears so that none might climb over; the great wooden doors turned on pivots, and once again snakes breathing fire and poison guarded them. But all who passed through on the Boat of Ra spoke the words of power decreed for that portal, and the doors swung open.

The Second Region was the Kingdom of Ra, and the gods

and heroes of old who had lived on earth when he was King dwelt there in peace and happiness, guarded by the Spirits of the Corn who make the wheat and barley flourish and cause the fruits of the earth to increase.

Yet not one of the dead who voyaged in the Boat of Ra might pause there or set foot on the land: for they must pass into Amenti, the Third Region of the Duat where the Judgement Hall of Osiris stood waiting to receive them.

So the Boat came to the next portals, and at the word of power the great wooden doors screamed open on their pivots – yet not so loudly did they scream as the man who lay with one of the pivots turning in his eye as punishment for the evil he had done upon earth.

Into the Third Region sailed the Boat of Ra, and here the dead disembarked in the outer court of the Judgement Hall of Osiris. But the Boat itself continued on its way through the nine other Regions of the Night until the re-birth of Ra from out of the mouth of the Dragon of the East brought dawn once more upon earth and the rising of the sun. Yet the sun would not rise unless each night Ra fought and defeated the Dragon Apophis who seeks ever to devour him in the Tenth Region of the Night.

The *Bais* of Setna and Se-Osiris did not follow the Boat of Ra further, but flew over the *Kas* of the newly dead who came one by one to the portal of the Hall of Osiris and one by one were challenged by the Door-Keeper.

'Stay!' cried the Door-Keeper. 'I will not announce thee unless thou knowest my name!'

'Understander of Hearts is thy name,' answered each instructed *Ka*. 'Searcher of Bodies is thy name!'

'Then to whom should I announce thee?' asked the Door-Keeper.

'Thou shouldst tell of my coming to the Interpreter of the Two Lands.'

'Who then is the Interpreter of the Two Lands?'

'It is Thoth the Wise God.'

So each *Ka* passed through the doorway and in the Hall Thoth was waiting to receive him, saying: 'Come with me. Yet why hast thou come?'

'I have come here to be announced,' answered the *Ka*.

'What is thy condition?'

'I am pure of sin.'

'Then to whom shall I announce thee? Shall I announce thee to him whose ceiling is of fire, whose walls are living serpents, whose pavement is water?'

'Yes,' answered the *Ka*, 'announce me to him, for he is Osiris.'

So ibis-headed Thoth led the *Ka* to where Osiris sat upon his throne, wrapped in the mummy-clothes of the dead, wearing the uraeus crown upon his forehead and holding the scourge and the crook crossed upon his breast. Before him stood a huge balance with two scales, and jackal-headed Anubis, god of death, stepped forward to lead the *Ka* to the judgement.

But before the Weighing of the Heart, each dead man's *Ka* spoke in his own defence, saying: 'I am pure! I am pure! I am pure! I am pure! My purity is as that of the Bennu bird, the bright Phoenix whose nest is upon the stone persea-tree, the obelisk at Heliopolis. Behold me, I have come to you without sin, without guilt, without evil, without a witness against me, without one against whom I have taken action. I live on truth and I eat of truth. I have done that which men said and that with which gods are content. I have satisfied each god with that which he desires. I have given bread to the hungry, water to the thirsty, clothing to the naked and a boat to him who could not cross the River. I have provided offerings to the gods and offerings to the dead. So preserve me from Apophis, the "Eater-up of Souls", so protect me – Lord of the Atef-Crown, Lord of Breath, great god Osiris.'

Then came the moment which the evil-doer feared but the good man welcomed with joy. Anubis took the heart out of the *Ka* that was the double of his earthly body and placed it in the Scale; and in the other Scale was set the Feather of Truth. Heavy was the heart of the evil-doer and it dragged down the Scale: lower and lower it sank, while Thoth marked the angle of the beam – until the Scale sank so low that Amemt the Devourer of Hearts could catch the sinner's heart in his jaws and bear it away. Then the evil-doer was driven forth into the thick darkness of the Duat to dwell with Apophis the Terrible in the Pits of Fire.

But with the good man the Feather of Truth sank down and his heart rose up, and Thoth cried aloud to Osiris and the gods, 'True and accurate are the words this man has spoken. He has not sinned; he has not done evil towards us. Let not the Eater-up of Souls have power over him. Grant that the eternal bread of Osiris be given to him, and a place in the Fields of Peace with the followers of Horus!'

Then Horus took the dead man by the hand and led him before Osiris, saying, 'I have come to thee, oh Unnefer Osiris, bringing with me this new Osiris. His heart was true at the coming forth from the Balance. He has not sinned against any god or any goddess. Thoth has weighed his heart and found it true and righteous. Grant that there may be given to him the bread and beer of Osiris; may he be like the followers of Horus!'

Then Osiris inclined his head, and the dead man passed rejoicing into the Fields of Peace there to dwell, taking joy in all the things he had loved best in life, in a rich land of plenty, until Osiris returned to earth, taking with him all those who had proved worthy to live for ever as his subjects.

All these things and more the *Bai* of Se-Osiris showed to the *Bai* of his father Setna; and at length he said, 'Now you know why I wished your fate to be that of the poor man and not of the rich man. For the rich man was he in whose eye the pivot of the Third Door was turning – but the poor man dwells for ever in the Fields of Peace, clad in fine robes and owning all the offerings which accompanied the evil rich man to his tomb.'

Then the two *Bais* spread their golden wings and flew back through the night to Thebes. There they re-entered their bodies which their *Kas* had been guarding in the Temple of Osiris, and were able to return to their place as ordinary, living father and child, in time to see the sun rise beyond the eastern desert and turn the cliffs of Western Thebes to pink and purple and gold as a new day dawned over Egypt.

The Tale of the Two Brothers

ONCE upon a time there were two brothers called Anpu and Bata who lived beside the Nile. Anpu the elder had a beautiful wife, and a house with a garden round it, and rich land beside the river. Bata the younger lived with them, more like a son than a brother. But he worked hard and willingly for Anpu, making his clothes, driving his oxen out to pasture, ploughing and sowing the seed in the rich mud after the Inundation, and reaping the golden corn as spring-time turned into the first hot days of summer. And in time he grew to be an excellent farmer: there was not his equal in the land, and Harmachis, the god of the rising sun, had him in his especial care.

Day by day Bata followed the oxen, and in the evening came back to the house laden with the herbs of the field, with milk and with wool, and with all the rest of the farm produce. And he would put them down before his elder brother who would be sitting there with his wife beside him; and he would eat and drink, and then go to sleep near the oxen to guard them from all harm. And when morning came he would take the bread he had baked and lay it before them before taking his own with him out into the fields as he drove the cattle to pasture.

As he walked behind the cattle one day, they spoke to him, saying, 'The best grass for us is over there!' And Harmachis gave him the power of understanding their words, so that he took them always to the best pastures, and the cattle grew exceedingly strong and beautiful, and had a multitude of fine calves.

For some time Bata and Anpu dwelt thus happily together, and the blessing of Harmachis that was upon all that Bata did brought prosperity such as few mortals have known.

Yet at last evil came out of it. For Anpu's wife grew jealous of Bata and envious that all their good fortune depended on him, and she brought trouble between the two brothers with lying tales and wicked sinful words. And the end of it was that on an evening of spring when Bata came home driving the herd before him, and carrying on his head a load of herbs as was his custom, the foremost cow turned and said, as she entered the stable before him, 'See, your elder brother is standing behind the door with a drawn knife in his hand to slay you. Therefore flee away.'

At first Bata paid no attention. But when the next cow said the same thing, he looked down and saw his brother's feet beneath the stable door. Then he cast down his load and fled away, with Anpu after him, knife in hand.

Then Bata cried out to Harmachis, god of the rising sun,

saying: 'My good lord who saves the good from the evil, help me now!'

Harmachis heard his cry and suddenly opened a channel of water between the two brothers which they could not cross since it was full of crocodiles. So they were forced to wait, one on either side, until the sun rose.

And when Harmachis had filled the world with the red light of morning, Bata cried to Anpu, 'Why did you run after me to slay me without waiting to hear what I had to say to you? Am I not truly your brother, and have you not been to me as a father and your wife as a mother?' And then he told all the tale of the wicked plots of Anpu's wife, and made a vow before Harmachis that what he had said was true, and cut himself with his knife to sanctify the oath.

Then Anpu was filled with sorrow, and longed to go and comfort his brother and beg his forgiveness: but he could not do so because of the channel full of crocodiles which Harmachis had opened between them.

Presently Bata said, 'Because you have believed evil of me and tried to kill me without letting me speak, I will leave you to tend your own cattle. And I shall go into the secret Valley of the Acacia, and there I shall call forth my *Bai*, my hidden soul, and place it on top of the acacia flowers. If anyone cuts down the acacia tree my *Bai* will fall to the ground, and you must come to seek it and put it in a cup of pure, cold water, so that it may return to my body once more and I may live. And you shall know that I have need of you and that the acacia has been cut down by this sign: when someone sets a cup of beer in your hand and the beer seethes in the cup and is troubled – then come in haste to seek me.'

So Bata journeyed across the desert to the Valley of the Acacia. But Anpu went back to his house, slew his wicked wife and flung her body to the dogs. Then he sat down and mourned for the loss of his younger brother.

Many days passed, and Bata still dwelt in the Valley of the Acacia. There he lived altogether alone, hunting the wild beasts in the desert and coming back each evening to lie down and sleep under the acacia which held his *Bai* upon its topmost bough. In time he built for himself a high tower in the Valley of the Acacia and filled it with good things so that it might be his home.

Now from time to time the gods themselves walked visibly in the Valley of the Acacia, and it chanced on a day that the nine who had highest honour at Memphis came to the tower where Bata dwelt.

When he saw them, Bata fell down and worshipped them. Then they spoke one to another about him, and at last Harmachis said: 'Greetings to you, Bata! Do you dwell here alone?' And when Bata bowed his head at this, Harmachis continued, 'We know that you left your home on account of the wife of your brother Anpu – the wicked wife whom he has now slain. And we hold that you have done well, and shown yourself truly innocent.'

Then Harmachis turned to Khnemu the moulder of men and said, 'It is good that Bata the righteous should dwell no more alone: make for him a woman to be his wife.' So Khnemu took clay and fashioned it and made the most beautiful woman in all Egypt, perfect in shape and limb. And Ra breathed the breath of life into her, and the rest of the gods gave her gifts. Then they departed to their own place, and the seven Hathors came to spin the fate of Bata's wife: and one of them said, 'She will die a sharp death.'

Bata rose from his knees when the Hathors had gone and took his lovely wife by the hand, and led her into the tower. And there he gave her jewels and garments of golden net, and she dwelt happily with him and he loved her exceedingly.

Presently Bata began to go hunting again during the day. But before he left his wife he told her of how his *Bai* dwelt in the topmost flower of the acacia tree beside the tower, and what would chance to him if any man should find it. Also he said to her, 'It has been revealed to me that trouble will come upon us from the river. So I command you to remain in the tower, and beneath the tree in the Valley of the Acacia, and never to go out of the valley to the shore lest the river should seize you.'

Bata told her this many times, and the more he told her the more she longed to go out of the Valley of the Acacia, and look upon this strange thing called the river. At last she could control her curiosity no longer, and one day when Bata was far away hunting in the desert, she stole out of the Valley of the Acacia and down to the river bank where she walked on the fresh grass, marvelling at the broad blue waters that danced and sparkled in the sunshine and rippled against the bank.

Presently, however, Hapi the Nile-god beheld her and was filled with desire. With a roar he came rushing down over the land to seize her, and she fled away towards the Valley of the Acacia crying aloud in terror. But as she turned to fly Hapi caught hold of her and before she could break away he snatched a lock of her hair.

Bata's wife fled back to the tower and never again ventured out of the Valley of the Acacia down onto the shore of the Nile; nor did she tell her husband of her disobedience or of how she had been punished for it.

But the Nile carried the lock of hair down to the sacred lake at Memphis, and it floated in the water at the place where the washermen from the palace washed the clothes of Pharaoh – and the sweet scent from the lock of hair passed into Pharaoh's garments.

Everyone marvelled at the perfume, which was sweeter and pleasanter than any that had ever been known before, and the washermen quarrelled among themselves, each claiming that he was responsible for giving Pharaoh this new and exquisite pleasure.

The overseer of the washermen was angry at these quarrels, and he went himself to the sacred lake to see if he could solve the mystery. He stood at the exact spot where the lock of hair was floating, and when he had seen it and smelt its fragrance he carried it in triumph to Pharaoh.

Then the scribes and magicians of Memphis were summoned into the presence of Pharaoh; and when they had studied the lock of hair, the Chief Magician said: 'O Pharaoh – life, health, strength be to you! – this is a wondrous lock of hair that comes from the head of a daughter of Harmachis, god of the rising sun. The essence of every god is in her. It comes to you from a distant land to bring you praise and good fortune. And therefore we advise you to send out messengers to seek for her and bring her to be your wife.'

'What you tell me fills my heart with delight and longing,' said Pharaoh. 'Therefore it is my decree that messengers go forth into all lands to find this daughter of Harmachis whom the gods have destined to be my bride.'

So messengers set out, each with a small company of soldiers to guard him, and they went far and wide in search of the princess with the scented hair. One party came at length to the Valley of the Acacia, and would have taken Bata's wife to be the bride of Pharaoh. But Bata drew his sword and smote them all to the ground in his anger.

Yet one man lived, though sore wounded, and crept away to tell Pharaoh. Then Pharaoh sent an army: but he bade them wait by the river while guile was tried. They obeyed his order and lay hidden in their boats while one woman went up into the Valley of the Acacia and spoke with Bata's wife. And when she told her of the power and glory that would be hers, as Pharaoh's bride, and gave her the rich jewels and ornaments that he had sent her, Bata's wife did not hesitate to run away secretly and sail down the Nile in the Royal Boat to become the bride of Pharaoh.

When she came to Memphis, Pharaoh loved her exceedingly and made her Princess of Egypt, the chief of his wives. But he said, 'My messengers report that you already have a husband in the Valley of the Acacia: tell me concerning him.'

And she said, 'All that needs to be told is that he is not as other men are. Therefore send swiftly to the Valley of the Acacia and cut down the acacia tree beside the tower, and destroy it utterly.'

Pharaoh issued the command. His servants hastened up the Nile far to the south until they came to the entrance to the Valley of the Acacia. They entered the Valley and cut down the tree which stood beside the tower and destroyed it with fire. And when the flower which held the *Bai*, the soul of Bata, was cut down it fell to the ground and Bata also sank down and died in that same moment of evil.

That very hour Anpu his brother entered his own house, washed his hands, and called for a cup of beer. A servant set it in his hands, and at once the beer grew muddy and seethed in the cup like a troubled sea.

Then Anpu cried, 'Evil has befallen Bata my brother! Now I must hasten away to the Valley of the Acacia to restore him.' So he bound his sandals on his feet, took his weapons and his staff and set out immediately.

In time he came to the Valley of the Acacia, entered the tower and found Bata lying there dead upon the floor. He wept and mourned for a while. Then he went out into the Valley of the Acacia and sought for the *Bai* of his brother. For three years he sought in vain, and at last he said, 'Tomorrow I will return to Egypt!'

When the sun rose he decided to spend one last day seeking for his brother's soul. All day he searched in vain, and as the sun was sinking he returned to the tower. As he passed beneath the branches of the new acacia tree which had grown where the old one stood a seed fell at his feet. He picked up the seed and flung it into a cup of cold water. Then he sat down according to his custom.

Now that seed held the *Bai* of Bata, and when it had sucked up all the water, Bata's body began to tremble all over; and presently the corpse sat up, ghastly in the moonlight, and held out its withered hand. Anpu set the cup in the corpse's hand, and it raised it to its lips and drained it. Then the soul returned into Bata's body, and he was a withered corpse no longer but a living man. He rose from where he lay, and the two brothers clasped each other in their arms – and the night fled away in the joy of their reunion.

But when the first light of dawn appeared and Harmachis the god of the morning was about to drive the chariot of Ra up into the sky beyond the eastern desert, Bata said to Anpu, 'I must leave you now, for so the gods decree. My human form cannot endure, and my spirit must enter into a bull, sacred to Ptah, Lord of Memphis. When the sun rises you will see me no more as Bata but only as this holy bull with all the correct marks upon me – never a black hair save upon my forehead, my neck and my back in spots of the right shape. You must mount upon my back and I will carry you to Pharaoh's court where you will be rewarded with silver and gold because you bring the bull who will become a great marvel throughout all the land – for all will deem that in it dwells the spirit of a god.'

Anpu embraced his brother once more, and then Bata went out into the darkness. And when the sun rose and the world was filled with light, there stood before the tower a magnificent white bull with great sweeping horns.

Anpu mounted on his back, and they travelled along the river bank for many days until they came to Memphis.

Pharaoh rejoiced when he saw the Bull and rewarded Anpu richly, saying, 'This is indeed a great wonder which has come to pass!' The whole land rejoiced at the coming of the great Bull of Ptah, and he was given a beautiful dwelling place and many attendants not far from the royal palace.

Anpu, laden with riches, returned to his home and dwelt there with all honour. Not long after he had gone from the Court, however, there was a holy day in honour of Ptah, and the great Bull passed into the Temple and stood in the holy place. Presently the Princess of Egypt came to make her offering, and the Bull said to her, 'Behold me alive, whom you thought dead!'

'Who then are you?' she asked in surprise, and the Bull answered, 'I am Bata your husband, whom you sought to kill by causing Pharaoh to cut down and destroy the tree in the Valley of the Acacia on which my spirit rested. But my brother Anpu found my *Bai* in the likeness of a seed, and now it has entered into this body and I Bata am the Bull of Ptah.'

The Princess was filled with fear and she fled speedily out of the Temple devising in her heart how she might destroy Bata the Bull even more thoroughly than she had destroyed him when he was a man and her husband.

At length she invited Pharaoh to her place. He came with the morning sun, and all day she entertained him and made his heart glad. At night they feasted, and she so wrought upon Pharaoh that he cried, 'Truly, my Princess, I will grant you a great boon, even to the half of my kingdom. Ask, and I will give!'

Then the Princess said, 'You must swear before the gods in these words: "Whatever you, the Princess of Egypt, ask, that I promise to grant."'

Pharaoh swore the oath. Then the Princess cried, 'Give me the liver of the Bull of Ptah to eat – for he is wholly useless for any kind of work.'

Pharaoh was filled with sorrow at her words. But for his oath's sake he needs must do as she asked. So next day he decreed a great feast in the Temple of Ptah, and commanded that the Bull should be slain as an offering, and one of the chief royal slaughterers was brought to kill the Bull. And after the deed was done and the attendants were carrying the body out of the Temple to prepare for the great feast, the dead Bull suddenly jerked his head and two drops of blood fell one on either side of the pylon gateway.

Next morning two persea trees had grown from the drops of blood and stood overshadowing the pylon gate, wonderful and fragrant. Then messengers hastened to the palace and told Pharaoh, 'Behold a wonder has come to pass. Two great persea trees have sprung up in the night and stand on either side of the Temple gateway, before the pylons.'

Then Pharaoh and all the people rejoiced greatly and paid much honour to the two magic trees.

They flourished for many months, and seemed to be bringing many blessings on the land of Egypt, not the least of which was that the Princess was soon to bear a child: for although Pharaoh had many children, only the child of the Great Royal Wife, the Princess of Egypt, could succeed to the throne.

When the time drew near, Pharaoh and the Princess went in state to the Temple of Ptah, and he wore the Double Crown of Egypt and the Princess was garlanded with flowers. After the ceremony they sat in the shade of the magic persea trees without the pylon gate.

Now Pharaoh slept for a while, and while he did, the persea tree behind her spoke to the Princess, saying, 'O wicked and deceitful one, know that I am Bata your husband whom twice you have slain – when my *Bai* rested on the tree in the Valley of the Acacia, and when it entered into the holy Bull of Ptah.'

Then the Princess was filled with fear, and she thought swiftly how she might slay Bata once and for all.

Soon she hit upon a plan. She cast herself at Pharaoh's feet, clasping his knees, and cried out: 'Pharaoh, my lord, grant me a boon – or I shall die, and no son will be born to sit on the throne of Egypt after you have gone up to dwell with Osiris!'

Then Pharaoh woke in a great fright and exclaimed, 'I swear before the gods to grant whatever you may wish – only rise from the ground and cease to cry out lest some evil befall both you and our unborn child.'

'Then cut down these persea trees!' she cried. 'Cut them into planks and use the wood. But burn with fire both the leaves and the roots.'

Pharaoh was filled with sorrow at her words, but he knew that he must not cross her will, and he could not break his oath.

So he sent for his carpenters and they cut down the persea trees and hewed them into planks, and burnt both the roots and the leaves.

The Princess of Egypt stood watching, and suddenly she laughed with joy at the destruction of the trees. As she laughed a splinter of wood from one of them flew into her mouth, and she swallowed it.

That night a son was born to her who grew into a strong and handsome young man. Pharaoh loved him well and made him the Prince of Kush so that all might know that he would be the next to sit upon the throne of Egypt.

And when Pharaoh went to join the other gods, the Prince became Pharaoh indeed. And at once he sent for all his lords, for the Princess his mother, and for Anpu. And he told them all that had befallen, saying: 'I am Bata, who has been born again, as the son of the good god who rests with Osiris and of this woman, who was my wife when I dwelt in the Valley of the Acacia.'

Then all bowed before him, crying: 'Pharaoh! Pharaoh! Pharaoh! Life, health, strength be to you!'

After this, judgement was passed upon the Princess of Egypt according to the law of gods and men, and she died a sharp death even as the Hathors had prophesied. But Bata reigned

Tales of Adventure

The Story of the Shipwrecked Sailor

WHEN Pharaoh Amen-em-het ruled Egypt in about the year 2000 B C he brought peace and prosperity to a country that had been torn by civil war and rebellion for nearly two hundred years. During his reign adventurers and traders went on many expeditions to the south – either up the Nile through Nubia and even as far as Ethiopia, or along the Red Sea and out into the Indian Ocean to the mysterious land of Punt, whence they brought back jewels and spices and other treasures.

The Royal Court, whether it was in residence at Thebes or Memphis, was thronged with ships' captains and the leaders of expeditions, each with a tale to tell – and each anxious to win a commission from Pharaoh to command some royal venture on the strength of his past achievements.

One day such a wanderer stopped the Grand Vizier in the palace courtyard at Thebes, and said to him, 'My lord, harken to me a while. I come with costly gifts for Pharaoh, nor shall his counsellors such as yourself be forgotten. Listen, and I will tell you of such adventures as have not been told: Pharaoh himself – life, health, strength be to him! – will reward you for bringing to his presence a man with such adventures to tell. I have been to a magic island in the sea far to the south – far beyond Nubia, to the south even of Ethiopia. I beg of you to tell Pharaoh that I am here and would tell my tale to him.'

The Grand Vizier was accustomed to such appeals, and he looked doubtfully at the wanderer and said, 'It seems to me that you speak foolishly and have only vain things to tell. Many men such as you think that a tall story will win them a commission from Pharaoh – but when they tell their tale they condemn themselves out of their own mouths. If what you have to tell is one of these, be sure that I shall have you thrown out of the palace. But if it is of sufficient interest, I may bring you before Pharaoh. Therefore speak on at your own risk, or else remain silent and trouble me no more.'

'I have such a tale to tell,' answered the wanderer, 'that I will risk your anger with an easy mind. When you have heard it, you will beg me to come before Pharaoh and tell it to him — even to the good god Pharaoh Amen-em-het who rules the world. Listen, then.

'I was on my way to the mines of Pharaoh in a great ship rowed by a hundred and fifty sailors who had seen heaven and earth and whose hearts were stronger than lions. We rowed and sailed for many days down the Red Sea and out into the ocean beyond.

'The captain and the steersman swore that they knew the signs of the weather and that the wind would not be strong but would waft us gently on our way. Nevertheless before long a tempest arose suddenly and drove us towards the land. As we drew near the shore the waves were eight cubits in height and they broke over the ship and dashed it upon the rocks. I seized a piece of wood and flung myself into the sea just as the ship ran aground: a moment later it was smashed to pieces and every man perished.

'But a great wave raised the board to which I clung high over the sharp rocks and cast me far up the shore, on level sand, and I was able to crawl into the shelter of the trees out of reach of the cruel, angry sea.

'When day dawned the tempest passed away and the warm sun shone out. I rose up to see where I was, giving thanks to the gods for my delivery when all the rest had perished. I was on an island with no other human being to be a companion to me. But such an island as no man has seen! The broad leaves of the thicket where I lay formed a roof over my head to shield me from the burning midday sun. When I grew hungry and looked about for food, I found all ready for me within easy reach: figs and grapes, all manner of good herbs, berries and grain, melons of all kinds, fishes and birds for the taking.

'At first I satisfied my hunger on the fruits around me. And on the third day I dug a pit and kindled a fire in it on which I made first of all a burnt offering to the gods, and then cooked meat and fish for myself.

'As I sat there comfortably after an excellent meal I suddenly heard a noise like thunder. Nearly beside myself with terror, I flung myself on the ground, thinking that it was some great tidal wave come to engulf the island: for the trees were lashing as if at the breath of the tempest and the earth shook beneath me.

'But no wave came, and at last I cautiously raised my head and looked about me. Never shall I forget the horror of that moment. Moving towards me I saw a serpent thirty cubits long with a beard of more than two cubits. Its body was covered with golden scales and the scales round its eyes shaded off into blue as pure as lapis lazuli.

'The serpent coiled up its whole length in front of where I lay with my face on the ground, reared its head high above me, and said: "What has brought you, what has brought you here, little one? Say, what has brought you to my island? If you do not tell me at once I will show you what it is to be burnt with fire, what is it to be burnt utterly to nothing and become a thing invisible. Speak quickly, I am waiting to hear what I have not heard before, some new thing!"

'Then the serpent took me in his huge jaws and carried me away to his cave, and put me down there without hurting me. Yes, though he had held me in his sharp teeth he had not bitten me at all: I was still whole.

'Then he said again, "What has brought you, what has brought you here, little one? Say what has brought you to this island in the midst of the sea with the waves breaking on all sides of it?"

'At this I managed to speak, crouching before him and bowing my face to the ground as if before Pharaoh himself.

' "I sailed by command of Amen-em-het, Pharaoh of Egypt, in a great ship one hundred and fifty cubits in length to bring treasure from the mines of the south. But a great tempest broke upon us and dashed the ship upon the rocks so that all who sailed in her perished except for myself. As for me, I seized a piece of wood and was lifted on it over the rocks and cast upon this island by a mighty wave, and I have been here for three days. So behold me, your suppliant, brought hither by a wave of the sea."

'Then the serpent said to me, "Fear not, fear not, little one, nor let your face show sadness. Since you have come to my island in this way, when all your companions perished, it is because some god has preserved and sent you. For surely Amen-Ra has set you thus upon this island of the blessed where nothing is lacking, which is filled with all good things. And now I will tell you of the future: here in this isle shall you remain while one month adds itself to another until four months have passed. Then a ship shall come, a ship of Egypt, and it shall carry you home in safety, and at length you shall die in your own city and be laid to rest in the tomb which you have prepared.

' "And now I will tell you of this island. For it is pleasant to hear strange things after fear has been taken away from you – and you will indeed have a tale to tell when you return home and kneel before Pharaoh, your lord and master. Know then that I dwell here with my brethren and my children about me; we are seventy-five serpents in all, children and kindred. And but one stranger has even come amongst us: a lovely girl who appeared strangely and on whom the fire of heaven fell and who was turned into ashes. As for you, I do not think that heaven holds any thunderbolts for one who has lived through such dangers. It is revealed to me that, if you dwell here in

patience, you shall return in the fullness of time and hold your wife and children in your arms once more."

'Then I bowed before him, thanking him for his words of comfort, and said, "All that I have told you is true, and if what you have said to me happens indeed, I shall come before Pharaoh and tell him about you, and speak to him of your greatness. And I will bring as offerings to you sacred oils and perfumes, and such incense as is offered to the gods in their temples. Moreover I shall tell him of all the wonders of this isle, and I shall sacrifice asses to you, and Pharaoh shall send out a ship filled with the riches of Egypt as presents to your majesty."

'The king serpent laughed at my words, saying, "Truly you are not rich in perfumes – for here in this island I have more than in all the land of Punt. Only the sacred oil which you promise me is scarce here — yet you will never bring it, for when you are gone this island will vanish away and you shall never more see it. Yet doubtless the gods will reveal it in time to come to some other wanderer."

'So I dwelt happily in that enchanted island, and the four months seemed all too short. When they drew to a close I saw a ship sailing over the smooth sea towards me, and I climbed into a high tree to see better what manner of men sailed in it. And when I perceived that they were men of Egypt, I hastened to the home of the serpent king and told him. But he knew already more than I did myself, and said to me, "Farewell, brave wanderer. Return in safety to your home and may my blessing go with you."

'Then I bowed before him and thanked him, and he gave me gifts of precious perfumes — of cassia and sweet woods, of khol and cypress, of incense, of ivory and of other precious things. And when I had set these upon the ship and the sailors would have landed, the island seemed to move away from them, floating on the sea. Then night fell suddenly, and when the moon shone out there was no island in sight but only the open waves.

'So we sailed north and in the second month we came to Egypt, and I have made haste to cross the desert from the sea to Thebes. Therefore, I pray you, lead me before Pharaoh, for I long to tell him of my adventures and lay at his feet the gifts of the King of the Serpents, and beg that he will make me commander of a royal ship to sail once more into the ocean that washes the shores of Punt.'

When the wanderer's tale was ended, the Grand Vizier laughed heartily, crying, 'Whether or not I believe your adventures, you have told a tale such as delights the heart of Pharaoh — life, health, strength be to him! Therefore come with me at once, and be sure of a rich reward: to you who tell the tale, and to me who brings before him the teller of the tale.'

So the wanderer passed into the presence of the good god Pharaoh Amen-em-het, and Pharaoh delighted in the story of the shipwrecked sailor so much that his chief scribe Ameni-amen-aa was set to write it down upon a roll of papyrus where it may be read to this very day.

The Adventures of Sinuhe

In spite of all that he had done to unite Egypt and bring peace and prosperity to her after years of civil war, Pharaoh Amen-em-het went in constant danger from plots to murder him, hatched by one great lord or another who wished to seize his throne.

Fearing lest one of these plots should prove successful, and knowing that if one of his lords tried to usurp the throne it would plunge Egypt into civil war again, Amen-em-het promoted his son Sen-Usert (whom the Greek historians called Sesostris) to be his viceroy and co-ruler, so that he should be ready to step into his place as Pharaoh immediately it became vacant, and be able to put down any rising or rebellion that might break out.

Amen-em-het's wisdom was proved ten years later when he was in fact murdered as the result of a conspiracy in the palace.

Sen-Usert was abroad at the time, leading an army against Temeh in Libya. He had defeated the enemy and was returning to Egypt with much booty and many captives, when messengers arrived by night – obviously bearing important news for the Prince.

Among Sen-Usert's chosen body-guard of 'Royal Companions' was a young warrior called Sinuhe who knew rather more than he should about the plot against Amen-em-het. When he saw the messengers, Sinuhe guessed that they must have tidings of what had happened at Thebes, and he crept silently up to the back of the royal pavilion and stood there as if on guard. But with his dagger he made a slit in the material where it was stretched over one of the posts so that he could hear everything that was said inside.

Sinuhe heard the messengers telling Sen-Usert of his father's death, and that he was now Pharaoh. 'You must ride for Thebes at once,' they said. 'Do not tell the army what has happened, but set out immediately with only the Royal Companions. Other messengers have gone to your faithful governors throughout Egypt commanding them to hide the news of the death of Pharaoh Amen-em-het from the people until Pharaoh Sen-Usert – life, health, strength be to him! – is proclaimed in Thebes.'

When Sinuhe heard all this he was filled with fear. If he went to Thebes with Sen-Usert and the Royal Companions his part in the plot to murder Amen-em-het might be discovered; and if he asked to remain with the army he might be suspected – and Sen-Usert would certainly realize that he had been spying and overheard the secret news.

Perhaps none of these things would have happened, but Sinuhe was seized with such panic that he slipped quietly out of the camp, to wait until he saw which way the army was marching. Then he crept down and made his way south along the edge of the desert, trying to avoid all towns and even villages. When he came to where the Nile begins to branch out into the many streams of the Delta he was in more danger of being seen. One man whom he met unexpectedly turned and fled, thinking that he was a bandit; and he came at evening to a district of islands and high reeds which must have been somewhere near where the modern city of Cairo now stands.

Here he found an old boat without oars or rudder, and as the wind was blowing from the west he trusted himself to it and drifted downstream towards Heliopolis, but came to the eastern bank of the Nile a mile or so outside the town.

So he continued on his way, crossing the isthmus of Suez near the Bitter Lakes and stealing by night across the frontier and into the Desert of Sinai. Here he nearly died of thirst, and indeed had given up all hope and lain down never to rise again, when he heard the lowing of cattle.

Creeping on his hands and knees, so weak was he, Sinuhe came to a camp of Asiatic nomads. The sheikh of the tribe recognized him as an Egyptian and guessed by his appearance that he was a man of importance. So he tended him carefully, feeding him gradually with milk and water until he was strong enough to take more solid food.

After this Sinuhe came without further adventures to the ancient city of Byblos in Syria where Egyptians had always been welcome since the great temple had been built on the spot where Isis found the body of Osiris in the column of King Malcander's palace.

He dwelt there for some time, and then journeyed further east to the great valley beyond the Lebanon range where King Ammi-enshi ruled the land which was then called Retenu. Ammi-enshi welcomed him, saying. 'Come and dwell in my country: I have other men of Egypt who serve me, and you will at least hear your native language in this place. Moreover it seems to me that you must have been a man of some importance in Egypt: therefore, tell me why you have left your home. What news is there from the court of Pharaoh?'

Then Sinuhe said, 'Pharaoh Amen-em-het has departed to dwell beyond the horizon; he has been taken up to the place of the gods – and I fled, fearing civil war in Egypt and danger to those who had been near to Pharaoh. I left Egypt for no other reason but this: I was faithful to Pharaoh and no evil was spoken against me. Yet I think that some god must have guided me and led me hither.'

'I have had news from Egypt since you left it,' said Ammi-enshi. 'The new Pharaoh is Sen-Usert the son of Amen-em-het. He has taken his place upon the throne of the Two Lands, he has set the Double Crown of Upper and Lower Egypt upon his head, his hands hold the scourge and the crook. There has been no rebellion yet in Egypt, but do you think that war will come?'

Sinuhe realized that Ammi-enshi was asking his advice as to whether it was safe to rebel against the rule of Egypt and seek to make Retenu an independent country outside the Egyptian Empire, and he said: 'If Sen-Usert is now Pharaoh, and all in Egypt are faithful to him, there will be no danger of rebellion or civil war. For Sen-Usert is a god upon earth, a general without an equal. He it was who led the army against the Libyans of Temeh and subdued them victoriously. He is a Pharaoh who will extend the frontiers of Egypt's empire: he will send his armies south into Nubia and east into Asia. Therefore my advice to you is that you send messengers to kiss the ground before him. Let him know of your loyalty, for he will not fail to do good to all lands that are true to him.'

Then King Ammi-enshi replied, 'How happy must Egypt be under so strong and great a Pharaoh! I will do even as you advise. But as for you, stay here with me and command my armies, and I will make you great.'

So Sinuhe prospered in the land of Retenu. He married the eldest daughter of the King and was given a palace to dwell in, upon an estate where all good things grew in abundance. There were groves of fig-trees and vineyards where grapes grew so thickly that wine was more plentiful than water; there were rich fields of barley and wheat, and pastures where the cattle grew fat. Never did Sinuhe know any shortage of roast meats, either beef or chickens from his lands, or the wild things which he hunted with his hounds on the lower slopes of Mount Lebanon.

Sinuhe did not gain all this for nothing. As commander of Ammi-enshi's army he made war on neighbouring tribes and peoples who tried to invade Retenu from the north and east – and in every venture he was successful, slaying the enemy with his strong arm and unerring arrows, carrying off the inhabitants as slaves and bringing back great droves of cattle to swell the royal herds.

So King Ammi-enshi grew to love him as if he were his son, and planned to make him next in succession to the throne by right of his wife, the Princess Royal: for it seems that either the King of Retenu had no sons or else the throne descended in the female line.

Not all the people of Retenu were pleased at the idea of being ruled in days to come by a foreigner, and there was a murmur of rebellion headed by a certain champion who was the strongest man and most famous warrior in the country, and against whom no one had been able to stand in battle.

When King Ammi-enshi heard of this, he was troubled at heart and sent for Sinuhe, saying to him, 'Do you know this man? Have you any secret that he has discovered?'

And Sinuhe answered, 'My lord, I have never seen him. I have never entered his house. He comes against me out of jealousy – and, if it pleases you, I will meet him in battle. For either he is a braggart who wishes to seize both my property and my power, or else he is like a wild bull who wishes to gore the tame bull and add his cows to his own herd. Or he is simply like a bull that can bear no other bull to be thought stronger or fiercer than he is himself.'

So the duel was arranged. It was to take place before a great gathering of the people of Retenu, in the presence of the King himself.

All night Sinuhe practised with his weapons, testing his bow and sharpening his javelins. At daybreak he came to the field of battle, and the people applauded him, crying, 'Can there be any fighting man greater than Sinuhe?'

But when the champion came striding out from among his followers, they fell silent: for he was a mighty man indeed.

He began the battle, shooting at Sinuhe with his arrows, and hurling his javelins. But Sinuhe was quick of foot and quick of eye, and he dodged them all or turned them harmlessly away with his shield.

Then he made ready for the champion, who came rushing on him waving a mighty battle-axe above his head. Sinuhe shot an arrow, and the champion turned it with his shield; then Sinuhe hurled a javelin so swiftly that the champion had no time to ward it off, but was struck in the neck by it, stumbled and fell upon his face. The battle-axe flew out of his hand: Sinuhe seized hold of it and smote off his rival's head at a single blow.

All the people of Retenu cheered him, and the King caught him in his arms and embraced him, crying, 'Surely here is the worthiest man in all the land to rule with me!'

So Sinuhe became the greatest lord in Retenu after Ammi-enshi, and ruled the land with him for many years, and became King after him when he died.

But when he grew old, Sinuhe began to long for his own land, and a great desire came upon him to see Egypt once more before he died and be laid to rest at last in a rock tomb at Thebes.

Pharaoh Sen-Usert knew that the new king of Retenu was that Sinuhe who had been his Royal Companion in the days of Amen-em-het; he had sent letters to him as to a loyal subject, and Sinuhe had replied as a loyal subject should.

Now he wrote begging to be forgiven for leaving the royal service at the time of uncertainty after Amen-em-het's death, and asking if he might return to Egypt to spend his old age there.

Sen-Usert wrote back at once, bidding him come to dwell in the Royal Palace as a great lord and trusted adviser, and he ended: 'Return to Egypt to look again upon the land where you were born and the palace where you served me so faithfully in the days before Osiris took to himself my father the good god Amen-em-het. You are now growing old, you are no longer a young man bent upon adventures. Look forward to the day of your burial: do not let death come upon you far away among the Asiatics. Dwell with me in Egypt, and when that day comes you shall be laid to rest at Western Thebes in a mummy case of rich gold with your face inlaid upon it in lapis lazuli. A sledge drawn by oxen shall bring you to your tomb while the singers go in front and the dancers follow behind until you come to the door of your sepulchre. That shall be made for you in the midst of the royal tombs where princes and viziers lie; and the walls shall be painted with all the wisdom of the dead so that your *Bai* shall pass safely into the Duat; and rich treasures and plentiful offerings shall be set in your tomb so that your *Ka* may feast upon them until the day comes when Osiris shall return to earth. Come quickly, for you grow old and you know not when some sickness may smite you down. It is not right that a noble of Egypt should be laid in the earth wrapped in a sheepskin like a mere Asiatic. Come quickly, for you have roamed too long!'

Sinuhe rejoiced exceedingly when he received this letter. At once he made arrangements to hand over the rule of Retenu with all his possessions to his eldest son; and then he set out for Egypt attended by a small party of his chosen followers.

When he reached the borders of Egypt he was met by an embassy from Pharaoh who welcomed him warmly and made much of the lords of Retenu who had come with him.

At the Nile a ship was waiting for him, and Sinuhe was brought up the river in great state and comfort to the palace of Pharaoh.

When he was led into the royal presence he prostrated himself on the ground before the throne and lay as if dead.

Then Pharaoh Sen-Usert said kindly, 'Lift him up and let him speak! Sinuhe, you have arrived at your home, you have ceased to wander in foreign lands and come back in honourable old age so that when the time comes you may be laid to rest in a fine tomb at Western Thebes and not thrust into the ground by Asiatic barbarians. See, I greet you by name! Welcome, Sinuhe!'

Then Sinuhe rose and stood before Sen-Usert with downcast eyes and said, 'Behold, I stand before you and my life is yours to do with as you will.'

Pharaoh stepped down from his throne and took Sinuhe by the hand. He led him to the Queen and said to her laughingly, 'See, here is Sinuhe, dressed like a wild Asiatic of the desert!'

Then the royal children came to greet him also, and Pharaoh uttered his decree, saying, 'I make Sinuhe a Companion of Pharaoh, a great lord of the Court. I give him such lands and riches as becomes such a one – those that he forfeited when he fled from Egypt long ago, and more than he lost, to welcome him on his return and show how happy we are to have him with us once more.'

And so Sinute became a great man in Egypt and a close friend of the Pharaoh from whom he had fled in a moment of panic. He gave lavish care to the carving and decorating of his tomb, and caused all the story of his adventures to be written on it, and also to be copied out and kept in the archives. And when he died he was laid to rest with all honour.

His tomb has not been found, but the account of his adventures has come down to us, for it was a favourite tale in Ancient Egypt and was written many times on papyrus and read for hundreds of years after his death.

The Peasant and the Workman

IN the days of Amen-em-het the Second, the son of Sen-Usert, there lived a peasant called Sekhti in the country near Lake Moeris south of Memphis. He had a wife and children, and he traded in all the produce of the countryside, which he carried to the city of Henenseten on his three donkeys.

One day, when he had gathered three full loads, he set out for Henenseten to sell them. The donkeys were laden with rushes and natron and salt, with wood and pods and seeds – all of which he had gathered in the country round about and which he knew would bring him much trade in the town.

When he drew near to Henenseten and came to the tow-path beside the canal, he found a man standing there whose name was Hemti, a workman who served Meruitensa, the High Steward of Pharaoh. He was a cruel and greedy man who held all peasants in contempt because they always spoke the truth and traded fairly, while he would cheat and lie and do anything to gain money and oppress those beneath him in rank.

As soon as he saw Sekhti coming across the desert, with the three asses laden with the fruits of his toil, he exclaimed, 'Oh, that some kind god of thieves would show me how to steal away the goods of Sekhti from him!'

Now Hemti's house stood by the canal, and the tow-path that ran beside it was no wider than the waist-cloth that a man wore folded about him. On one side was the deep water of the canal, and on the other side was Hemti's cornfield in which the corn was tall and close together, the ears just turning to gold as the time of harvest drew near.

Then Hemti had an idea. 'Run to the house!' he shouted to a servant. 'Bring me an embroidered sheet as swiftly as you can!'

The servant sped on his errand, and returned in a moment with the sheet, which Hemti spread on the tow-path so that one end dangled almost into the water and the other touched the nearest stalks of corn.

Now Sekhti approached along the path, which was a public thoroughfare open to all men, and the only way from Moeris to the city of Henenseten.

'Ho there!' shouted Hemti. 'Be careful you don't trample on my clothes!'

'I'll do my best,' answered Sekhti. 'I'll go as carefully as I can. But you haven't left very much room!'

Sekhti guided his asses along the edge of the corn, trying to avoid the sheet on the tow-path; but Hemti shouted, 'Keep out of my corn! Isn't the path good enough for you?'

'I'm going as carefully as I can,' answered Sekhti. 'I'm not trespassing in your cornfield on purpose, but your clothes are taking up most of the path and it's very difficult to get by.'

Sekhti certainly did his best. But as they brushed through the edge of the corn one of the donkeys began to help itself to the ripe ears, and Hemti shouted, 'You know the law! I can confiscate your ass if it eats my corn, and fine you for all the damage it does.'

'I've been as careful as I can,' answered Sekhti, 'but you've made it very difficult for me, blocking the tow-path like this. I had to take my asses over your ground to avoid your clothes and it's hardly fair to seize them for taking a couple of mouthfuls as they passed. I know who is the real owner of all this land: it is Meruitensa the High Steward of Pharaoh. He does justice upon all the robbers in this land – surely I shall not be robbed when passing through his domain?'

Said Hemti gleefully, 'I myself am the High Steward of this land, and the word of such as I will be accepted against that of a mere peasant.'

And he commanded his servants to seize all three donkeys

with their loads. Moreover he bade them lay Sekhti on the ground and beat him with rods of green tamarisk. Sekhti wept and cried aloud, for he was in great pain.

'Keep silent, Sekhti,' counselled Hemti, 'or I will send you to the Demon of Silence.'

'You beat me, and you steal my goods, and now you would take away even my voice,' groaned Sekhti. 'If you now restore my goods, I will cease from crying out, and say nothing about the violence you have offered me.'

But Hemti laughed at him and refused to return either the asses or their loads. At last Sekhti went away into Henenseten to the house of Meruitensa to seek for justice. He found the High Steward coming out of the door of his house to embark in his boat on the canal and go to the Hall of Judgement. Sekhti fell upon the ground before him and cried, 'Justice, my lord! Give me justice against Hemti who has robbed me!' And with that he poured out his story.

'Prepare your plea, and come tomorrow into the Judgement Hall,' said Meruitensa when he had heard all. He bade his servants to give Sekhti food and shelter for the night and he went on his way.

After the cases had been heard in the Hall of Judgement, Meruitensa told the other lords there assembled about the case of Sekhti.

'We know that Hemti is grasping,' they said. 'But why should we punish him for taking a handful of natron and a pinch of salt from a mere peasant? Nevertheless, let this Sekhti state his case in due form tomorrow.'

The next day accordingly Sekhti came into the Hall of Judgement and began to make his plea to Meruitensa.

'O my Lord Steward, greatest of the great, guide of the needy! May good fortune attend you wherever you may go! May you sail whither you will and not see the face of fear! May the fish come into your nets and the plump waterfowl likewise! For you are a father to those that are orphaned, you are the widow's husband, the desolate woman's brother, the garment of the motherless. Let me sing your praises throughout the land, for you are a very fount of virtue – a guide without greed, a great one who is never mean, one who destroys deceit, encourages justice, and hears the words of the most humble of your petitioners. Therefore let me speak and give me true justice. Put an end to my oppression, restore that which has been stolen from me!'

Sekhti continued with words such as these for a long time, while the scribes wrote them down. At last Meruitensa said, 'I will consider your case and hear more from you tomorrow. This night I have given orders that you shall be fed at my house.'

Then Meruitensa hastened into the presence of Pharaoh Amen-em-het and said, 'O Pharaoh – life, health, strength be to you! – I have found a peasant called Sekhti who has such a gift of words that it is wonderful to listen to him. He has been robbed and defrauded by that wicked miser Hemti, but I have passed no judgement until I had told you all and you had heard his words.'

When the scribes had read out all that Sekhti had said, Pharaoh clapped his hands with delight and cried, 'Never have I heard such words of praise! You did right to tell me of them, for they give me great joy. Now, as you love me, lengthen out his complaint: do not reply to his charges but see how long he will continue with such speeches – and be sure that all he says is written down and brought to me.'

So each day Sekhti was summoned to the Hall of Judgement, and he spoke a rich stream of words, praising Meruitensa, praising Pharaoh, wishing them all imaginable joys in this life and all good fortune in the long journey through death.

Each evening as the day's speeches were read to him Pharaoh marvelled more and more that a peasant should have such eloquence. And he urged Meruitensa to drag out the trial still longer. But he said also, 'Make sure, Meruitensa, that Sekhti is provided with four loaves and two measures of beer each day – though do it through a friend so that he does not know that it comes from you. And send to his home to see that his wife and children lack for nothing. Then take down his words, and bring them to me, for they delight my heart.'

On the sixth day Meruitensa caused Sekhti to be beaten with rods, though lightly. And for the next three days the peasant had this further outrage to complain about and beg to have avenged in more and more flowery language.

'O my Lord Steward!' Sekhti was still protesting on the ninth day, 'you destroy deceit and encourage justice; you raise up every good thing and crush all evil; even as plenty comes to drive out famine, as clothing covers nakedness, as the clear sky after a storm brings warmth to those who are cold, as fire cooks that which is raw, as water quenches the thirst of those who have been lost in the desert – even so is your justice and your mercy: therefore look upon me with kindness, bring me content, do me right and not evil, give me justice for what I have suffered wrongfully.'

Then at last Meruitensa bade two men raise Sekhti from the ground and bring him out of the Hall of Judgement. Sekhti feared that he was going to be punished for having troubled the High Steward for nine long days, but Meruitensa said, 'Fear not, Sekhti, for what you have done. Your speeches have been reported to Pharaoh and they delighted his heart. Come now before him and you shall be satisfied and all your goods shall be restored.'

And the end of it was that not only did Pharaoh cause all the three asses with their loads to be restored to Sekhti, but he gave him all that belonged to Hemti and made him chief workman and guardian of the canal in his place. He sent to bring Sekhti's wife and five children to dwell at Henenseten, and he made the cruel, proud Hemti into a peasant and set him to work on the shores of Lake Moeris.

But Sekhti was beloved of Pharaoh more than any other of the overseers of his royal works, and he dwelt in the shadow of the palace with all his household and grew rich and famous.

The Taking of Joppa

In the days of Thutmose III, the Pharaoh who reigned in Egypt after the Great Queen Hatshepsut, an expedition set out to capture and punish the city of Joppa in Palestine which had rebelled against him. In command of the expedition was the great general Thuti who was the trusted friend and Royal Companion of Pharaoh. And to show that he came as Pharaoh's representative he brought with him the great royal sceptre, a golden mace called 'Beautiful-in-Strength'.

Thuti camped outside Joppa, a mile or so from the city, which was surrounded with great walls, all heavily fortified. Very soon he realized that to conquer the city by force of arms was almost impossible and that to reduce it by laying siege might take months or even years.

It seemed to Thuti that Joppa was only to be taken by guile. So, when he had made his plans, he sent a herald with a message asking the Governor of Joppa to meet him next day midway between the city and the camp.

The Governor agreed readily to this, and during the night Thuti caused a great pavilion to be pitched on the level sand half a mile from the camp and the same distance from the great gate of Joppa. There were no trees or bushes anywhere about, and there seemed to be nowhere in the pavilion where enough men could hide to raise suspicions of treachery. But nonetheless Thuti had prepared all that he needed for his great attempt in the two hundred baskets that stood ready packed along the back wall of the silken pavilion.

When the Governor of Joppa arrived, Thuti welcomed him under a canopy spread in front of the entrance to the pavilion. But first he led him inside so that he could see that no armed men were hiding there.

Then the Governor's guard withdrew to a little distance, Thuti sent his own handful of attendants out of earshot, and the two sat down under the canopy to drink their wine and discuss the situation.

They talked for a long time, each making offers which the other refused; and as they talked the Governor drank more and more of the strong wine of the south while Thuti saw to it that his cup was never empty for long.

When he felt that the Governor's wits were becoming a little dazed, Thuti said to him, after looking suspiciously all round the pavilion to make sure that no one could possibly overhear him, 'My friend, it seems to me that I can only take the city after a siege of two years. If I take so long, Pharaoh will be angry and take away my rank and riches: for the cost of keeping a large enough army to surround Joppa for two years will be very great – and Thutmose does not like to spend money, but rather to hoard it. And if I go back to him now and say that Joppa is too strong to take by assault, and can only be reduced by a two-year siege, he will be angrier still, and may even take away my life.'

Thuti paused, and the Governor became interested. 'What do you suggest?' he asked eagerly.

'Pharaoh has always been a hard master to me,' said Thuti, 'and I am sure that you will be a kinder and more generous one . . . It is in my mind to betray Pharaoh's cause and join you in revolt against him.'

'I swear by Jahwah, my god, that you shall be second only to myself in the new kingdom which we shall carve out of Pharaoh's domains!' cried the Governor. Then he paused doubtfully, and added, 'But how am I to know that you do not mean to trick me? If I open my gates to your army as to friends, may not these friends become enemies once they are inside my walls?'

'I have thought of that,' answered Thuti. 'We are sensible

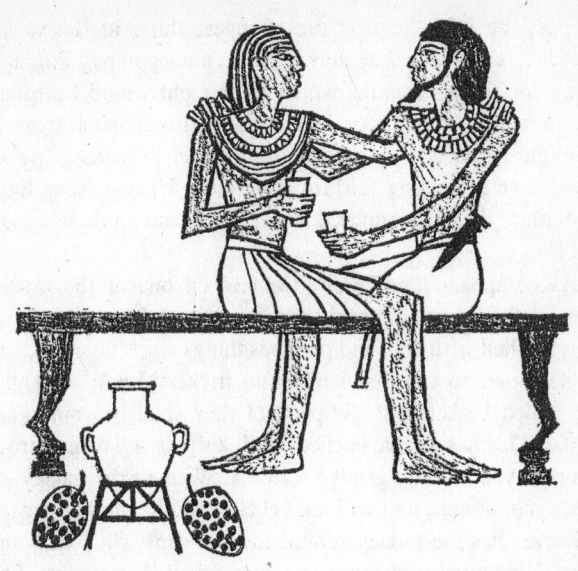

men: we know that oaths can be broken, so I will swear none to you. We know that loyalty and honour are but empty words, so I will not speak of them. But I will give you a greater surety than any of these.'

'Yourself?' interrupted the Governor eagerly. 'Yes. If you give yourself up to me, I will trust your word. For a man's own life is the only thing of real value to him.'

'I would willingly give myself up to you here and now,' said Thuti. 'But if I did so, how do we know that Pharaoh's army will not cast me off to die in your hands, elect a new general and attack Joppa? No, I have a better surety still: me you may take after you have taken that. Come, and I will show you.'

He led the Governor into the pavilion and pointed to the baskets ranged along the wall.

'See,' he said, 'here is the strongest thing in the world: gold! In these sealed baskets is all the money to pay Pharaoh's army for the six months which *he* thought would be enough for the whole expedition. And in them also are such treasures as might be needed for other purposes such as bribing friendly princes or rewarding faithful governors. I came from Egypt with more than two hundred such baskets and all these remain. See!'

As he spoke Thuti broke the seal on one of the baskets, opened the lid and showed the Governor of Joppa that it was indeed filled with gold and precious things.

'To prove to you that I mean no trickery I will send all of the sealed baskets into Joppa, and they shall be yours absolutely. This one I have opened I will keep as my own share: I am sure you will not grudge it to me. Without the money, the army cannot exist and will not rebel or set up another general. Whoever has the money commands the army. So I will summon four hundred of my men – men whom I can trust. They will come before us unarmed, as you will see, and carry the baskets into Joppa. You will send your chariot before them to bear the news and cause the gates to be opened in readiness, but you yourself will remain with me until you and I have seen the treasure carried into the city. Then I will speak to the army and tell the men of what has chanced, and they will be faithful to you – you who will then have the money to pay them.'

All this seemed very straightforward and satisfactory to the Governor. Like most Asiatics he saw nothing unusual in an army and its general changing sides, particularly if paid well enough to do so. And he could see no way in which Thuti might be cheating him.

So he agreed to the plan, and instructed his charioteer, saying, 'Drive ahead of the bearers until you come to the great gates of Joppa. Then bid them open and lead the bearers with their loads into the city, crying: "Rejoice! For Jahwah has given Thuti and all that is his into our hands. Behold here the vanguard of his tribute!"'

Then Thuti summoned four hundred of his men who came before them unarmed and picked up the baskets, two men to each basket, and carried them slung on poles thrust through their handles.

When they had started on their way across the open desert towards Joppa, the Governor said suddenly: 'Thuti, my friend, it was told to me that you had brought with you Pharaoh's sceptre which is called "Beautiful-in-Strength". It is said that magic goes with it and the might of Pharaoh. Will you not therefore touch me on the brow with it and set it in my hands, and then bow down before me as your new lord?'

'That will I do willingly,' answered Thuti, his eyes flashing suddenly. 'Come into the pavilion where the precious sceptre is hidden.'

So they went into the pavilion and Thuti drew out the golden mace 'Beautiful-in-Strength' from its hiding place and showed it to the Governor who was so lost in awe and admiration that he fell on his knees before it.

'Touch me on the forehead with it,' he cried, 'and give me the power that goes with it!'

'Look at me, Governor of Joppa and enemy of Pharaoh Thutmose – life, health, strength be with him!' cried Thuti. 'Thus Amen-Ra the great god of Egypt gives him victory over a traitor!'

So speaking, he struck the Governor on the head with 'Beautiful-in-Strength' and crushed his skull at a single blow.

Then he went back to the entrance of the pavilion and stood there in the shadow of the canopy, quietly buckling on his armour as he watched the bearers draw near and enter into Joppa.

For the charioteer who went ahead had cried aloud to the

watchmen on the gate: 'Rejoice, for we have overcome Thuti the Egyptian: his army is our army, and in these two hundred baskets come the vanguard of his tribute – all the gold and precious things which Pharaoh sent to pay his troops!'

So the four hundred unarmed men entered into Joppa and set down the baskets in the gateway. Speedily they broke the seals and opened the lids of the baskets. And out of each basket sprang an armed man, and in each basket were arms and weapons for the men who had carried the baskets.

The people of Joppa were taken by surprise, and the six hundred armed Egyptians were easily able to capture and hold the great gate until Thuti and his army reached it and marched into the city.

So Joppa fell in one day, and Thuti sent a letter to Pharaoh saying: 'Rejoice, for Amen-Ra your father has delivered the Governor of Joppa into your hands along with his city and all his people! Send men to carry away the spoils and lead captive male and female slaves to fill the House of Amen-Ra! Send men to occupy Joppa and hold it for you for ever more!'

Thuti continued on his way after the capture of Joppa, and brought all the lands round about under Egyptian rule. Then he returned to Pharaoh, and Thutmose heaped honours and riches upon him, and gave him a great golden bowl which may still be seen with its inscription to 'Thuti, the Follower of Pharaoh in every country, the trusted Follower of Pharaoh, the Commander of Garrisons, the Overseer of the Northern Countries, the trusted man of Pharaoh in every foreign country and the islands which are in the midst of the Sea; he who fills the storehouses with lapis lazuli, silver and gold; the Commander of the Army – praised by the Pharaoh of the Upper and Lower lands, Thutmose Ra-men-Kheper – even the Royal Companion, Thuti.'

The Story of the Greek Princess

In the days when Seti II, the grandson of Rameses the Great, was Pharaoh of Egypt, there came a great ship driven by a storm from the north, which sought shelter in the Canopic mouth of the Nile.

Near the place where the ship anchored stood the temple of the ram-headed god Hershef, who watched over strangers. If any man took sanctuary in the shrine of Hershef, he was safe from all his enemies; and if a slave knelt before the statue and vowed to serve the god, he became free from his master.

The ship which had come to Canopus was reported at once to Thonis, the Warden of that mouth of the Nile, and he learnt that it belonged to a prince of the people whom the Egyptians called the People of the Sea, or the Aquaiusha – that is the Achaeans, those who dwelt in Greece and the islands of the Aegean and in Ionia, whom we now call the Mycenaeans.

Thonis discovered this from a group of the sailors on the ship who, when they learnt of what chanced to those who sought sanctuary in the Temple of Hershef, deserted in a body and asked to be allowed to serve the god. When Thonis asked them why they wished to leave their master, since it seemed strange to him that men of the Aquaiusha should wish to enter the service of an Egyptian god rather than return to their homes, they replied that they feared the vengeance of their own gods if they remained on the ship.

For it seemed that the Prince their master had carried off the wife of one of the kings of Greece, together with much of his treasure – and this after the Greek king had received him as a guest and friend, and entertained him kindly in his palace.

Thonis was as much shocked as the sailors by this behaviour – for in Egypt as in Greece to behave thus to one's host was thought to bring a sure vengeance from the gods. And he seized the Prince's ship with all on it and guarded it closely until he learned the will of Pharaoh. But the Greek Princess he caused to be escorted with all honour to the Temple of Hathor, the goddess of love and beauty.

When Seti heard of all this, he commanded Thonis to bring the ship, with all who had sailed in her, up the Nile to Memphis.

All was done as he commanded, and when they arrived the Princess was placed for safety in the Temple of Hathor at Memphis. But the Prince was led at once before Seti where he sat in his great hall of audience.

'O Pharaoh, life, health, strength be to you!' cried Thonis, kissing the ground before Seti's feet according to custom. 'I bring before you this stranger, a prince of the Aquaiusha, that you may learn from his own mouth who he is and why he has come to your shores.'

Then Seti spoke kindly to the stranger Prince, saying, 'Welcome to the land of Egypt, if you come in peace and as one who serves the gods. My Warden of the Nile, Thonis, tells me that in your own land you are the son of a king. Tell me of that land of that king – for it is my delight to hear strange stories and tales of other lands.'

The handsome young Prince in his bronze armour that shone like gold bowed before Pharaoh and said, 'My lord, I come in peace – driven here against my will by the god of the sea whom we call Poseidon. I am the son of Priam, the great King of Troy, and I have been on a visit to Greece where I have won to be my wife the most beautiful woman in the world – Helen, Princess of Sparta, and daughter of its King, Tyndareus.'

Seti the Pharaoh looked thoughtfully at the proud young Prince, and said, 'Tell me, Prince of Troy, how did you come to win this Princess of Sparta? Do the kings of the Aquaiusha send their daughters across the sea to be wedded to the princes of other lands? For my learned scribe Ana, here, tells me that the city of Troy is far across the water from the land and islands of the Aquaiusha, and that there is war and rivalry between the two lands.'

'Then your scribe Ana is in error,' answered the Prince loftily. 'There was some fighting in my grandfather's day, but since then we have dwelt at peace. I came as one of the many princes of the Aquaiusha who were suitors for the hand of fair Helen – and King Tyndareus of Sparta gave her to me.'

At this the sailors who had sought sanctuary in the Temple of Hershef murmured, and Seti the Pharaoh said to them, 'Thonis reports that you who are now servants of Hershef tell another tale concerning these matters. Speak without fear, for you are now my subjects, and I will protect you.'

'King of Egypt,' answered the leader, 'we few sailors come from the islands and are of the Greek people, whom you call Aquaiusha, not men of Troy, whom we hold to be barbarians. We serve the gods of Greece – and we fear them also and know that they punish wrongdoing.

'This man, Prince Paris of Troy, who was our master, came as he says as a friend to Sparta. But he does not speak the truth of what happened there. All the people of our lands have heard of Helen, the most beautiful woman in the world the daughter of King Tyndareus of Sparta and Ledz his Queen – though it is said that in truth Zeus, King of the Gods, whom you call Amen-Ra, was her father.'

Seti nodded when he heard this and murmured, 'Even as Amen-Ra was the father of Hatshepsut, the Great Queen of Egypt. Yes, the gods can indeed be the fathers of the spirits that dwell in the bodies of kings and queens.'

'The princes of Greece and of the islands all sought the hand of Helen in marriage,' went on the sailor, 'not only for her beauty but also because whoever married her would become the King of Sparta. But Paris of Troy was not among their number. No, King Tyndareus gave his daughter to Menelaus, the younger son of the King of Mycenae, and made all the rest of her suitors swear to abide by his choice and to stand by Menelaus should anyone strive to steal his wife.

'That was several years ago. Since then Tyndareus has made Menelaus King of Sparta and he has reigned there with Helen as his Queen. The Prince of Troy came as a guest and an ambassador, and was welcomed as such. He dwelt at Sparta for many days, until Menelaus was forced to leave the city for a while on some affair of state. When he was gone, Paris carried off Helen by force, together with much treasure, and sailed away – only to be caught in a storm sent by the angry gods and driven hither.'

'That is false!' shouted Prince Paris angrily. 'Helen came of her own free will – she begged me to take her, for she hated her husband, Menelaus! And the treasure we took with us was her own.'

'Prince of Troy,' said Seti the Pharaoh, 'you have already told me two tales which do not agree. First you say that you won this princess from her father when all the princes of the Aquaiusha came as her suitors, and then you admit that you took her from the husband whom her father had chosen for her and made King of Sparta . . . Vizier, lead this prince of Troy with all honour to the Royal Guest-House – and see that he and his followers are well guarded and ready to appear before me again when I command their presence.'

'Pharaoh has spoken – life, health, strength be to him!' cried Para-em-heb the Vizier, prostrating himself before Seti. Then at a sign from him the guards closed in and led the Prince of Troy and his followers away.

'And now,' said Seti the Pharaoh, 'we will visit this princess of the Aquaiusha where she dwells in the Temple of Hathor.'

Seti and his companions, the scribe Ana* and Roi the High

* Ana was the author of *The Tale of the Two Brothers*.

Priest of Amen-Ra, made their way to the Temple of Hathor where the lovely Princess Helen had been lodged in the care of the priestesses of the goddess.

When he beheld her, Seti felt that he was indeed in the presence of the loveliest woman in the world, perhaps even of a goddess upon earth.

The tale of the Princess was far different from that of the Prince. According to her, she had dwelt in great happiness with her husband Menelaus and her two children, and felt no love at all for Paris the Trojan. Indeed, from what she told him, Seti understood that Paris had carried her off by magic, taking upon himself the shape of Menelaus to lure her away from the palace, down the long valley to the sea and away in the ship which had so soon been caught by the storm.

Such shape-shifting was familiar among the magicians of Egypt, though it seemed from Helen's words that only the gods practised it in Greece, and that magic was hardly known in her country.

'Therefore, great Pharaoh,' begged Helen, 'protect me in honour here until my lord and love Menelaus comes to seek and claim me from you – and do not let this evil prince carry me as a shameful captive to Troy.'

Helen wept, and the great red jewel she wore, the Star Stone which the goddess of love had given her, seemed to weep tears of blood as it trembled on her bosom in the dazzling sunlight that fell between the columns.

Seti was much moved by her tale, and he swore an oath to her, saying, 'By Amen-Ra, Father of Gods and Men, I swear that here in the Temple of Hathor you shall dwell with all honour until Menelaus comes for you. And I will send away this evil Prince of Troy without his treasure or his captive – and if he strives to steal you again, he shall meet his death, and any of his nation who come to Egypt seeking you stand in danger of death also.'

All things were done as Pharaoh Seti commanded. The Prince of Troy raged and threatened in vain. The treasure he had stolen was taken from him and set in Pharaoh's treasury until Menelaus should come to claim it; and Paris was told that he must depart forthwith in his ship down the Nile before sunrise on the next day.

'I will depart indeed!' he shouted when Pharaoh's messenger brought him the royal command. 'But it will be up the river to rescue my wife from those who would keep her from me!'

Yet before the sun rose the Trojan ship was speeding down the river below Heliopolis, and ere the next sun rose it was out on the Great Green Sea, heading northwards towards Troy on the outskirts of the world.*

All this came about very strangely, or so any of the Aquaiusha would have thought: but to the people of Egypt it was not at all out of the ordinary.

On the night before the Prince of Troy set sail, Pharaoh Seti's daughter Tausert knelt in prayer in the Temple of Hathor, for she was High Priestess of that goddess. As she knelt it seemed to her that the temple shook and a great light shone behind her. Turning she beheld the shape of Thoth himself, the great god of wisdom and messenger of Amen-Ra.

'Fear not,' said Thoth as Tausert fell on her face before him. 'I come hither to work the will of the most high god Amen-Ra, father of us all – and by his command you, who shall one day be Queen of Egypt, must learn of all that is performed this night so that you may bear witness of it in the days to come, when that king of the Aquaiusha who is the true husband of Helen shall come to lead her home.

'Know then that it is the will of Amen-Ra that the Aquaiusha, amongst whom he is worshipped by the name of Zeus, shall fight a great war for Helen which shall last for ten years

---

* The people of Egypt knew certainly of no land further away than the great island of Kefti which the Greeks called Crete.

and end only when the city of Troy lies in ruins. For the beauty of Helen shall it be fought – for an empty beauty, since here Helen remains until Menelaus comes. But this night I, whom the Aquaiusha name Hermes the Thrice Great, must draw forth the *Ka*, the double of Helen, the ghostly likeness of her that shall deceive all eyes and seem to Paris and to all at Troy to be none other than the real woman. For the *Ka* of Helen and not for Helen herself shall the great war of Troy be fought, and the will of the Father of Gods and Men shall be accomplished.'

Then Thoth passed out of the shrine towards the cell where Helen dwelt. And presently the light shone in the shrine once more and Tausert saw him pass through it followed by the *Ka* of Helen – so like Helen herself that none could tell the difference. Thoth leading the way, they passed through the closed door of the temple and so onwards through the night until they reached where the ship lay at the quay-side below Memphis. And there Thoth, taking on the form of Hermes by which Paris would know him, delivered the *Ka* of Helen into his hands. And, rejoicing greatly, Paris cast off the mooring ropes and set sail northwards for Troy.

Yet Helen dwelt still in the Temple of Hathor at Memphis. And as the years passed most of the Egyptians forgot how she had come there, and many worshipped her as Hathor come to earth in human form, and most spoke of her as the Strange Hathor.

In time Seti died. His spirit went to dwell in the Hall of Osiris and his body was laid to rest in a great tomb below the Valley of Kings in Western Thebes. There was then a time of trouble in Egypt when various of his sons struggled for the throne. But at length Set-nakhte wore the Double Crown and held the scourge and the crook – and his half-sister Tausert sat by his side as Queen of Egypt.

Set-nakhte did not reign for long, and when he too was

gathered to Osiris, his son the third Rameses became Pharaoh of Egypt.

All this while Helen had dwelt in the Temple of Hathor at Memphis and, though it was nearly twenty years since Paris had brought her to Egypt, she seemed scarcely to have aged at all but was still more lovely than any other woman in the world.

Now both Seti and Set-nakhte had faithfully observed the oath made to her. But young Rameses was of a different metal, and as soon as he became Pharaoh he declared that he would marry Helen and make her his Queen.

'She may be only a Princess of the Aquaiusha,' he declared. 'She may long ago have been the wife of one of the kings of that people – but she is still the loveliest of women, and she shall be mine!'

In vain Queen Tausert tried to persuade him against so wicked a deed. 'I care nothing for what my father and my grandfather may have sworn,' he cried. 'I have sworn no oath, except one, to marry Helen!'

'But,' urged Tausert, 'suppose her husband King Menelaus is still alive?'

This troubled Rameses a little, and he waited before marrying Helen until his chief magicians had looked into the matter for him.

While they were doing so, there came a shipwrecked sailor up the river to Memphis and knelt at the shrine of Hathor to pray for help. Tausert was still the High Priestess of Hathor, and now that her son was Pharaoh, she had returned to dwell in the Temple. So when she saw the sailor kneeling in the shrine, she went to ask him whence he came and why he had come to the Temple of Hathor instead of that of Hershef, where strangers usually sought sanctuary.

'I come in obedience to a dream,' answered the man. 'Hermes, whom you call Thoth, visited me as I slept and bade me seek the Strange Hathor in her temple at Memphis and tell all my tale without hiding anything.'

'Speak on,' answered Tausert, 'and fear nothing. The Strange Hathor sits hidden in the shrine and hears all that you tell me.'

'Then know,' said the sailor, 'that I am Menelaus, King of Sparta. Troy fell several years ago, and since then I and my ships have been blown hither and thither about the seas. At length I came in my ship to the mouth of the River of Egypt, and with me was my wife the beautiful Helen, whom Paris stole and to rescue whom the war was fought. My other ships anchored behind the Island of Pharos, but I sailed into the mouth of the Nile, and there my ship was struck by a sudden storm of wind and wrecked on a little island.

'We all escaped safely to the shore and sought shelter in some caves nearby. Helen and I were alone in one cave – and when I awoke in the morning she had vanished. All day we searched for her, but there was no trace. She could not have left the island, for the river ran deep and fierce all round it, and we could only think that she had strayed too near the water's edge and been carried away by a crocodile.

'I was in despair. To have fought for ten years at Troy to win back Helen; to have wandered on the sea for seven years trying to bring her home to Sparta – and then to lose her like this seemed unbearable. I was tempted to fall upon my own sword and seek her in the fields of asphodel where Hades reigns, whom you call Osiris.

'Then, as I lay mourning for my loss, Hermes appeared to me. "Do not despair, Menelaus," he said. "All that has chanced is by the will of Zeus. Helen is not lost to you – she never was found. In the morning a ship of the Egyptians will carry you to Memphis. There seek Helen in the Temple of the Strange Hathor. Enter the temple and tell all your tale to the priestess there – and you will find the true Helen."

'All this I have done. A ship came to the island next day and carried us up the river to Memphis – and here I kneel as Hermes bade me.'

'King of Sparta,' said Tausert solemnly, 'the will of Amen-Ra, whom you call Zeus, is accomplished. Seventeen years ago, in the days when the good god my father Seti Merneptah was Pharaoh, Paris the Prince of Troy was driven with his ship into the Nile, and Thoth the all-wise whom you call Hermes decreed that Helen should remain here in safety and honour until you came for her, and here she still dwells.'

'But Priestess,' gasped Menelaus, 'Helen went with Paris to Troy! We sacked Troy and I carried Helen away on my ship. She was with me until two days ago when she vanished from the island. How can she have been here ever since Paris stole her from my palace in Sparta?'

'By the will of Amen-Ra the *Ka* of Helen was drawn forth by Thoth and sent with Paris,' answered Tausert. 'For a double, a mere spirit form, did you of the Aquaiusha fight and Troy fall. Here is Helen!'

As she spoke Tausert drew back the curtains of the shrine and Helen stepped forth with outstretched arms – beautiful Helen, unsoiled by years of siege and wandering, or by the unwished love of Paris.

Like a man in a dream Menelaus took Helen in his arms and held her as if to feel whether she were shadow or woman.

'Helen!' he murmured. 'Did you dwell here through all these years while Paris carried a mere thing of air to Troy? Have we fought and died for a mere *eidolon*, a magic likeness, not a real woman? Truly the magic of the Egyptians is greater even than we have ever thought – and in Greece they are spoken of as the wisest of all men!'

Then Helen said: 'My lord and my love, we are not safe yet. Although I have dwelt here all these years honoured and unharmed, a great danger has come upon me suddenly. The

new Pharaoh, Rameses, the son of this lady, my protectress Tausert, wishes to make me his wife – and today he comes for his answer: whether I will be his willingly or by force.'

'This royal lady, Queen Tausert – does she favour the match?' asked Menelaus.

'So little,' replied Tausert, 'that I will do all in my power to help you both to escape from Egypt – provided no harm comes to Rameses my son.'

Then the three of them spoke together and devised a daring scheme.

At noon that day came Rameses the Pharaoh to the Temple of Hathor to claim fair Helen as his bride. He found her clad in mourning garments, with her hair hanging loose, while Menelaus, still ragged and unshaven as befitted a shipwrecked sailor, stood respectfully at a little distance, and Queen Tausert strove to comfort Helen.

'What has chanced here?' asked Rameses.

'That for which you prayed, my son,' answered Tausert. 'This man is a messenger whom you should welcome. He was a sailor who came from Troy in the ship of Menelaus of Sparta, that prince of the Aquaiusha who was husband to Helen. The ship in which he sailed was wrecked on the island of Pharos, and Menelaus is dead.'

'Is this true, stranger?' asked Rameses.

'O Pharaoh – life, health, strength be to you!' answered Menelaus, kneeling before him in the Egyptian manner. 'With my own eyes I saw him dashed on the rocks, and the waves carry his broken body out to sea.'

'Then, Helen, nothing stands between us!' cried Rameses.

'Only the memory of him who was my husband,' answered Helen.

'Your grief cannot be great after all these years.'

'Yet he was my husband, and a great king among my people the Greeks, and I would mourn him and pay due funeral rites to his memory so that his spirit may be at rest and dwell in the land where Hades rules. Wherefore I beg you to let me honour him as a king should be honoured – though his body is lost in the deep sea.'

'That I grant willingly,' said Rameses. 'You have but to command, and all shall be done as you wish. I know nothing of the funeral customs of the Aquaiusha, so you must instruct me.'

'I must have a ship,' said Helen, 'well furnished with food and wine for the funeral feast, and a great bull to sacrifice to the spirit of my husband. And I must have treasures also – those which Paris stole long ago from my husband's palace when he carried me away. This sailor here and his companions in shipwreck should accompany me, for they know all that should be done, and it will take many men to perform the sacrifice. I must accompany them to speak the words and pour the last offering to my husband's spirit – and all this must be done on the sea in which his body lies, for then only can his spirit find rest in the realm of Hades – and only then can I be your bride.'

In his eagerness to win Helen, Rameses agreed to all that she asked. A ship was loaded with the treasures that Seti had taken from Paris; the Greek sailors, Menelaus among them, brought the great sacrificial bull on board and took charge of it; Helen, clad in her mourning robes, stood in the prow of the ship, the sunlight flashing on the red Star Stone that she wore – and the ship sailed swiftly down the Nile and out on to the sea near Canopus.

But next day there came a messenger, stained with brine and the dust of travel, and knelt before Rameses, crying, 'O Pharaoh – life, health, strength be to you! – that sailor of the Aquaiusha who came with the news of the death of Menelaus was none other than Menelaus himself! When the ship was well out on the Great Green Sea beyond Canopus, the Aquaiusha sacrificed the bull indeed – but to the sea-god to give them a safe passage back to Greece. Then they seized us of Egypt who were on the ship and cast us into the sea, bidding us swim back to Memphis and tell you, O Pharaoh, that the will of Amen-Ra and of Thoth was accomplished and Helen, safe both from Paris the Trojan and from you, was on her way back to Sparta with her lawful husband, Menelaus.'

Now in his anger and disappointment Rameses wished to kill Tausert his mother, for he realized that she had known about Menelaus and had helped to rob him of Helen. But that night ibis-headed Thoth appeared to him and said, 'Pharaoh Rameses, all these strange happenings have been by the will of Amen-Ra the god and father of all Pharaohs. By his will Helen was brought to Egypt; at his command I drew forth her

Ka and sent it with Paris, to deceive him and all the Aquaiusha and the Peoples of the Sea; and he brought it about that Helen should be restored to her husband and sent to her home with him and with the treasures that Paris stole.'

Then Pharaoh Rameses bowed his head to the will of Amen-Ra and heaped greater honours yet upon his mother Queen Tausert, High Priestess of Hathor.

The Treasure Thief

RAMESES the Third, the Pharaoh who, when he first came to the throne, wished to marry Helen of Troy, ruled for many years and Egypt grew prosperous under him. Early in his reign he defeated invasions from both Palestine and Libya; but after this he lived at peace with his neighbours and encouraged trading to such an extent that he became the richest of all the Pharaohs.

Rameses gathered his treasures together in the form of gold and silver and precious stones – and the more he gathered the more anxious he became lest anyone should steal his hoards.

So he sent for his Master Builder, Hor-em-heb, and said to him, 'Build me a mighty treasure house of the hewn stone of Syene; make the floor of solid rock and the walls so thick that no man may pick a hole in them; and rear high the roof with stone into a tall pyramid so that no entrance may be broken through that either.'

Then Hor-em-heb, the Master Builder, kissed the ground before Rameses, crying, 'Oh Pharaoh! Life, health, strength be to you! I will build such a treasure house for you as the world has never seen, nor will any man be able to force a way into it.'

Hor-em-heb set all the stone-masons in the land of Egypt to work day and night quarrying and hewing the stone from the hard rock on the edge of the desert above Syene where the Nile falls from its most northerly cataract near the isle of Elephantinē. And when the stone was hewn, he caused it to be drawn on sledges down to the Nile and loaded on boats which bore it down to Western Thebes, where the temple of Rameses was already rising, which stands to this day and is now called Madinet Habu.

Under the care of the Master Builder the walls of the new building were reared and a pyramid was built over the whole, leaving a great treasure chamber in the middle. In the entrance he set sliding doors of stone, and others of iron and bronze; and when the untold riches of Pharaoh Rameses were placed in the chamber, the doors were locked and each was sealed with Pharaoh's great seal, that none might copy on pain of death both here and in the Duat where Osiris reigns.

Yet Hor-em-heb the Master Builder played Pharaoh false. In the thick wall of the Treasure House he made a narrow passage, with a stone at either end turning on a pivot that, when closed, looked and felt like any other part of the smooth, strong wall – except for those who knew where to feel for the hidden spring that held it firmly in place.

By means of this secret entrance Hor-em-heb was able to add to the reward which Pharaoh gave to him when the Treasure House was complete. Yet he did not add much, for very soon a great sickness fell upon him, and presently he died.

But on his death-bed he told his two sons about the secret entrance to the Treasure House; and when he was dead, and they had buried his body with all honour in a rock chamber among the Tombs of the Nobles at Western Thebes the two young men made such good use of their knowledge that Pharaoh soon realized that his treasure was beginning to grow mysteriously less.

Rameses was at a loss to understand how the thieves got in, for the royal seals were never broken, but get in they certainly did. Pharaoh was fast becoming a miser, and he paid frequent visits to his Treasure House and knew every object of value in it – and the treasure continued to go.

At last Pharaoh commanded that cunning traps and meshes should be set near the chests and vessels from which the treasure was disappearing.

This was done secretly; and when next the two brothers made their way into the Treasure House by the secret entrance to collect more gold and jewels, the first to step across the floor towards the chests was caught in one of the traps and knew at once that he could not escape.

So he called out, 'Brother! I am caught in a snare, and all your cunning cannot get me out of it. Probably I shall be dead by the time Pharaoh sends his guards to find if he has caught the Treasure Thief; if not, he is certain to have me tortured cruelly until I tell all – and then he will put me to death. And whether I live or die, he or one of the royal guards will recognize me, and then they will catch you, and you too will perish miserably – and maybe our mother also. Therefore I beg you, as you hope to pass the judgement of Osiris whither I am bound, that you draw your sword and strike off my head and carry it away with you. Then I shall die quickly and easily; moreover no one will recognize my body, so that you at least will be safe from Pharaoh's vengeance.'

The second brother tried to break the trap. But at last, realizing that it was in vain, and agreeing that it was better for one of them to die than both, and that if his brother were recognized their whole family might suffer, he drew his sword and did as he had begged him to do. Then he went back through the passage, closing the stones carefully behind him, and buried his brother's head with all reverence.

When day dawned Pharaoh came to his Treasure Chamber, and was astonished to find the body of a man, naked and headless, held fast in one of his traps. But there was still no sign of a secret entrance – for the Treasure Thief had been careful to remove all tracks – while it was quite certain that the seals on the doors had not been broken.

Yet Pharaoh was determined to catch the Treasure Thief. So he gave orders that the body should be hung on the outer wall of the palace and a guard of soldiers stationed nearby to catch anyone who might try to take it away for burial, or anyone who came near to weep and lament.

When the mother of the dead man heard that the body of her son was hanging on the palace wall and could not be given the sacred rites of burial, she turned upon her second son, crying, 'If the body of your brother remains unburied, his spirit cannot find peace in the Duat nor come before Osiris where he sits in judgement: instead he will wander for ever as a ghost, lost upon earth. Therefore you must bring me his body – or else I go straight to Pharaoh and beg for it by the love which he bore to your father Hor-em-heb his Master Builder. If he learns that you are the Treasure Thief, I cannot help it; but I will at least bury you with your father and brother in the great tomb of Hor-em-heb.'

At first her son tried to persuade her that the burial of the head was enough: for this he had set secretly where Hor-em-heb lay. And then he pointed out to her that it was surely better for one of her sons to lie unburied than for both of them to die. But she would not listen to him, and he was forced to promise to do his best to recover his brother's body.

So he disguised himself as an old merchant, loaded two donkeys with skins of wine, and set out along the road which ran by the palace wall. As he passed the place where the soldiers were encamped he made the donkeys jostle against each other, and he secretly made holes in the wine-skins which had bumped together as if some sharp pieces of metal on their harnesses had done it.

The good red wine ran out onto the ground, and the false merchant wept and lamented loudly, pretending to be so upset that he could not decide which of the skins to save first.

As soon as they saw what was happening, the soldiers of the guard came running to help the merchant – or rather to help themselves. This they proceeded to do until the two damaged skins were empty, and the wine was already on its way to their heads.

By this time the merchant had made friends with his gallant rescuers, and was so grateful to them for saving his wine from being wasted on the desert sand that he made them a present of another skin of wine, and sat down to share it with them. They did not refuse their help when yet another skin was broached; but before it was emptied they were past saying anything, and lay snoring on the ground with their mouths open.

Darkness was falling by this time, and the false merchant had no difficulty in taking down the body of his brother from the wall, wrapping it in empty wine skins, and carrying it away on one of his donkeys. Then, having cut a lock of hair from one side of each soldier's head, he went triumphantly home to his mother—and the funeral was completed before the morning.

When it was light and Pharaoh discovered that the body had gone, his rage was great, and he caused the guards to be

laid out and beaten on the feet with rods as a punishment for their drunkenness.

'Whatever the cost, I must have the Treasure Thief!' cried Pharaoh, and forthwith he invented a new plan to catch him. He disguised one of his own daughters, a royal Princess, as a great lady from a foreign land, and bade her camp before the city gates and offer herself in marriage to the man who could tell her the cleverest and wickedest deed he had done in the whole of his life.

The Treasure Thief guessed at once who the strange maiden was, and why she was asking these questions. But he was determined to outdo Pharaoh in cunning. So he went to visit the Princess just as the sun was sinking, and he carried with him, hidden under his cloak, the hand and arm of a man who had lately been executed for treason by command of Pharaoh.

'Fair Princess, I would win you to be my wife,' he said.

'Then tell me the cleverest and the wickedest things that you have ever done,' she answered, 'and I will say "yes" to your offer of marriage if they are wickeder and cleverer than any I have yet heard.'

As the sun went down behind the hills that hid the Valley of the Kings, the Treasure Thief told his tale to the Princess.

'And so,' he ended, 'the wickedest thing I ever did was to cut off my own brother's head when he was caught in Pharaoh's trap yonder in the secret chamber of the Treasure House; and the cleverest was to steal his body from under the noses of the soldiers who were set to guard it.'

Then the Princess cried out to the royal attendants who were hidden nearby as she seized the thief, saying, 'Come quickly, for this is the man Pharaoh is seeking! Come quickly, for I am holding him by the arm!'

But when Pharaoh's attendants crowded in with their lighted torches and lamps, the Treasure Thief had already slipped away into the darkness, leaving the dead man's arm in the

Princess's hands – and she saw how cleverly she had been tricked.

When Pharaoh Rameses heard of this further example of daring and craftiness, he exclaimed, 'This man is too clever to punish. The land of Khem prides itself on excelling the rest of the word in wisdom: but this man has more wisdom than anyone else in the land of Khem! Go, proclaim through the city of Thebes that I will pardon him for all that he has done, and reward him richly if henceforth he will serve me truly and faithfully.'

So in the end the Treasure Thief married the Princess and became a loyal servant of Pharaoh Rameses III. Nor did he ever have any further need to enter the Royal Treasure Chamber by the secret entrance made into it by Hor-em-heb the Master Builder.

The Girl with the Rose-red Slippers

In the last days of Ancient Egypt, not many years before the country was conquered by the Persians, she was ruled by a Pharaoh called Amasis. So as to strengthen his country against the threat of invasion by Cyrus of Persia, who was conquering all the known world, he welcomed as many Greeks as wished to trade with or settle in Egypt, and gave them a city called Naucratis to be entirely their own.

In Naucratis, not far from the mouth of the Nile that flows into the sea at Canopus, there lived a wealthy Greek merchant called Charaxos. His true home was in the island of Lesbos, and the famous poetess Sappho was his sister; but he had spent most of his life trading with Egypt, and in his old age he settled at Naucratis.

One day when he was walking in the market-place he saw a great crowd gathered round the place where the slaves were sold. Out of curiosity he pushed his way into their midst, and found that everyone was looking at a beautiful girl who had just been set up on the stone rostrum to be sold.

She was obviously a Greek with white skin and cheeks like blushing roses, and Charaxos caught his breath – for he had never seen anyone so lovely.

Consequently, when the bidding began, Charaxos determined to buy her and, being one of the wealthiest merchants in all Naucratis, he did so without much difficulty.

When he had bought the girl, he discovered that her name was Rhodopis and that she had been carried away by pirates from her home in the north of Greece when she was a child. They had sold her to a rich man who employed many slaves on the island of Samos, and she had grown up there, one of her fellow slaves being an ugly little man called Aesop who was always kind to her and told her the most entrancing stories and fables about animals and birds and human beings.

But when she was grown up, her master wished to make some money out of so beautiful a girl and had sent her to rich Naucratis to be sold.

Charaxos listened to her tale and pitied her deeply. Indeed very soon he became quite besotted about her. He gave her a lovely house to live in, with a garden in the middle of it, and slave girls to attend on her. He heaped her with presents of jewels and beautiful clothes, and spoiled her as if she had been his own daughter.

One day a strange thing happened as Rhodopis was bathing in the marble-edged pool in her secret garden. The slave-girls were holding her clothes and guarding her jewelled girdle and her rose-red slippers of which she was particularly proud, while she lazed in the cool water – for a summer's day even in the north of Egypt grows very hot about noon.

Suddenly when all seemed quiet and peaceful, an eagle came swooping down out of the clear blue sky – down, straight down as if to attack the little group by the pool. The slave-girls dropped everything they were holding and fled shrieking to hide among the trees and flowers of the garden; and Rhodopis rose from the water and stood with her back against the marble fountain at one end of it, gazing with wide, startled eyes.

But the eagle paid no attention to any of them. Instead, it swooped right down and picked up one of her rose-red slippers in its talons. Then it soared up into the air again on its great wings and, still carrying the slipper, flew away to the south over the valley of the Nile.

Rhodopis wept at the loss of her rose-red slipper, feeling sure that she would never see it again, and sorry also to have lost anything that Charaxos had given to her.

But the eagle seemed to have been sent by the gods – perhaps by Horus himself whose sacred bird he was. For he flew straight up the Nile to Memphis and then swooped down towards the palace.

At that hour Pharaoh Amasis sat in the great courtyard doing justice to his people and hearing any complaints that they wished to bring.

Down over the courtyard swooped the eagle and dropped the rose-red slipper of Rhodopis into Pharaoh's lap.

The people cried out in surprise when they saw this, and Amasis too was much taken aback. But, as he took up the little rose-red slipper and admired the delicate workmanship and the tiny size of it, he felt that the girl for whose foot it was made must indeed be one of the loveliest in the world.

Indeed Amasis the Pharaoh was so moved by what had happened that he issued a decree:

'Let my messengers go forth through all the cities of the Delta and, if need be, into Upper Egypt to the very borders of my kingdom. Let them take with them this rose-red slipper which the divine bird of Horus has brought to me, and let them declare that her from whose foot this slipper came shall be the bride of Pharaoh!'

Then the messengers prostrated themselves crying, 'Life, health, strength be to Pharaoh! Pharaoh has spoken and his command shall be obeyed!'

So they set forth from Memphis and went by way of Heliopolis and Tanis and Canopus until they came to Naucratis. Here they heard of the rich merchant Charaxos and of how he had bought the beautiful Greek girl in the slave market, and how he was lavishing all his wealth upon her as if she had been a princess put in his care by the gods.

So they went to the great house beside the Nile and found Rhodopis in the quiet garden beside the pool.

When they showed her the rose-red slipper she cried out in surprise that it was hers. She held out her foot so that they could see how well it fitted her; and she bade one of the slave girls fetch the pair to it which she had kept carefully in memory of her strange adventure with the eagle.

Then the messengers knew that this was the girl whom Pharaoh had sent them to find, and they knelt before her and said, 'The good god Pharaoh Amasis – life, health, strength be to him! – bids you come with all speed to his palace at Memphis. There you shall be treated with all honour and given a high place in his Royal House of Women: for he believes that Horus the son of Isis and Osiris sent that eagle to bring the rose-red slipper and cause him to search for you.'

Such a command could not be disobeyed. Rhodopis bade farewell to Charaxos, who was torn between joy at her good fortune and sorrow at his loss, and set out for Memphis.

And when Amasis saw her beauty, he was sure that the gods

Time Chart

(Approximate dates only until 1570 BC)

BC		
3200	DYNASTY I	Menes unites Upper and Lower Egypt.
2700	DYNASTY III	Zoser: Imhotep builds the Step Pyramid at Saqqara.
2600	DYNASTY IV	Khufu: the Great Pyramid at Giza. *The Golden Lotus; Teta the Magician*. Khafra: the Second Pyramid and the Sphinx. Menkaura: the Third Pyramid.
2080	DYNASTY XI	Beginning of the Middle Kingdom.
2000	DYNASTY XII	Amen-em-het I. *The Story of Sinuhe*. Amen-em-het II. *The Peasant and the Workman*.
1570	DYNASTY XVIII	Ahmose expels the Hyksōs and begins the New Kingdom.
1490–1468		Hatshepsut builds her mortuary temple at Der-el-Bahri.
1468–1436		Thutmose III builds first temple at Karnak. *The Taking of Joppa*.
1405		Thutmose IV uncovers the Sphinx.
1405–1367		Amen-hotep III builds temple at Luxor.
1347–1339		Reign of Tutankhamen.
1308	DYNASTY XIX	Rameses I.
1309–1291		Seti I.
1290–1224		Rameses the Great. *The Princess and the Demon; The Book of Thoth; Se-Osiris and the Sealed Letter; The Land of the Dead*.

1224–1214		Merneptah.
1214–1190		Seti II. *The Story of the Two Brothers* by Ana the Scribe.
1184		The Fall of Troy (traditional date).
1182–1151	DYNASTY XX	Rameses III. *The Greek Princess; The Treasure Thief.*
570–526	DYNASTY XXVI	Amasis. *The Girl with the Rose-red Slippers.*
c. 450	DYNASTY XXVII	(Persian.) Herodotus visits Egypt.
332–30	DYNASTY XXXI	(The Ptolemies.) Alexander the Great and his successors ruled Egypt.
30		Death of Cleopatra. Egypt then became a Roman province.

Also by Roger Lancelyn Green

THE ADVENTURES OF ROBIN HOOD

The tales of Robin Hood and his merry men in Sherwood Forest, which never cease to fire the imagination.

KING ARTHUR AND HIS KNIGHTS OF THE ROUND TABLE

The old stories of chivalry told afresh from the original sources, with beautiful scissor-cut pictures by Lotte Reiniger.

THE TALE OF TROY

The story of Helen, the Trojan war, and Odysseus's adventures on his long journey home to Greece.

TALES OF THE GREEK HEROES

The author has re-told the legends as the Greeks themselves thought of them, as the history of the Heroic Age.

THE LUCK OF TROY

When Nicostratus was two he and his mother, the beautiful Helen, were carried off by Prince Paris of Troy. Ten years later he vows to help the Greek army to capture Troy.

MYTHS OF THE NORSEMEN

A collection of all the surviving myths of the Norsemen, which in one continuous narrative reads with all the excitement and heroic feeling of one of the original sagas themselves.

A BOOK OF DRAGONS

A rich and exciting selection of the very best dragon stories from the time of the ancient Greeks to the present day.

Some other Puffins you might enjoy

THE VIKING SAGA

Henry Treece

A brilliant portrayal of this dramatic epoch of history, the three books that make up Henry Treece's breathtaking trilogy *Viking's Dawn, The Road to Miklagard* and *Viking's Sunset* are available separately and in one volume.

Into this magnificent epic is woven the true spirit of the Vikings, whose great urge for travelling the seas took them on incredible voyages in defiance of icy waters, terrible hardships and blood-thirsty resistance.

THE BONNIE PIT LADDIE

Frederick Grice

All his life Dick had expected to follow his father and brother into the coal mine. It seemed the only natural employment for boys in the pit village where he lived and he had never even questioned this way of life until the night he had to help home the owner of the mine. And he began to wonder by what right Mr Sleath lived so well and held such power over his workers' lives. But it took a bitter strike and a pit accident to make Dick break loose from the pit for his future.

DRAGON SLAYER

THE STORY OF BEOWULF

Rosemary Sutcliff

Lion-hearted Beowulf, the hero who had the strength of thirty men in his arms, sailed away over the whale road to rid the Danes of their deadly scourge, the prowling monster who struck terror into the bravest warriors of Denmark as they waited night after night in King Hrothgar's court. Great glory came to Beowulf before he died, the renown from his three great battles, with Grendel and his fearful mother, and with the dragon who guarded the brilliant treasure-hoard hidden away in the earth.

Rosemary Sutcliff's retelling of the Anglo-Saxon epic *Beowulf* grasps the splendour and mystery of the original poem. It is a story to feed the imagination powerfully, and fill the mind with a trembling awe.

THE BLUE HAWK

Peter Dickinson

The hawk was sick – something was terribly wrong, so Tron carried it out of the Temple on his wrist, and from that moment found that his future and the future of the Kingdom were bound up in the fierce, untamed spirit of the blue hawk, and he was plunged into an exciting adventure saga of secret passages, battles and dark intrigue.

Tron's world is set in a decaying civilization, with a dominating priesthood and a powerless king, and through it all runs the ancient force of the Gods whom they all serve.

This book won the *Guardian* award.

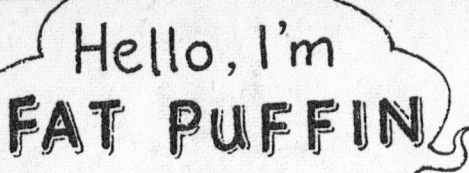